The Krankies Go Dogging
Jesamine James

Copyright© Jesamine James
Second paperback edition 2014.

The characters and events portrayed in this book are fictional.
Any similarity to real persons, living or dead, is coincidental and not intended by the author.

All rights reserved. No part of this book may be reproduced, stored in a retrieval system or transmitted without written permission of the publisher.

Content

Chapter 1   - Mum
Chapter 2   - Yahoo
Chapter 3   - Work
Chapter 4   - Wendy
Chapter 5   - Mission
Chapter 6   - Contact
Chapter 7   - Bob
Chapter 8   - Chase
Chapter 9   - Chips
Chapter 10 - Action
Chapter 11 - Down
Chapter 12 - Enough
Chapter 13 - Lesson
Chapter 14 - Quit
Chapter 15 - Move
Chapter 16 - Roast

Other books available by Jesamine James.
Janine, Eggs and Lemons (A Novella)
This is a novella.
When Emily Palmer finds herself in the waiting area of the labour ward with an irate mother-to-be, she recounts the story of how she happens to be there, alone, to calm the situation.
Her bizarre courtroom tale, of the oddest custody battle in history, gives her reason to reflect on the outcome of her child's future happiness on the small decision of her birth name.
Scrag - Up The Hill Backwards
"Even when I die, I'll come back to haunt you."
It's time for Jes to bury Marie's ghosts forever.
Six-year-old Marie finds her world has changed and become one of confusion, deceit and abuse.
No longer called by her birth name, she is unaffectionately referred to as Scrag - a shortened version of Scraggy-knickered-nut-rag.
Her will to survive manifests quite bizarre tactics, as she deviates off course into a childhood of insanity, paranoia, glue-sniffing, self-harming and messages from David Bowie ringing through her ears.
Her mind contrives strategies to cope with the continued onslaught that it seems destined to endure.
Adulthood is her escape route if she can survive the wait, but can demons be truly locked away in the past forever?
This is the story of one child's mind at the mercy of a real life monster.

Mum

Cas opened his mail at the kitchen table, as his mother cooked milk for the coffee. He was quite happy to have cold milk in his morning beverage, but the woman had her routine of boiling the milk in a small metal pan on the hob.

As it was the only thing she ever cooked, Cas never offered to take on the task himself. It wasn't that she couldn't cook, but she had fed the boy for fifteen years showing him every step of the process of preparing meat and vegetables and of course her famous Sunday roast. In return, for the following fourteen years of his life, it was his turn to cook. Although he was very good, his range was limited. His mother's palette was as routine as her milk pan, and when he had attempted to diversify the menu, she flatly refused to eat it.

Life had become a routine in itself for Cas. Daily he searched for jobs, made phone calls, opened rejection letters and on occasion attended an interview. It wasn't the way he'd envisaged it would be, as a small boy. Then, he'd dreamed of becoming things far beyond his reach like an astronaut or a pop star, but even his earliest memory of wishing to be an ice-cream man seemed beyond his grasp these days. His efforts in finding a job, resulted in either rejection or being completely ignored. It didn't get him down anymore. It was how it was and would probably always be that way.

Expecting a normal Friday morning, no different from the day before or the week before, Cas tore open the next letter, glanced through it and slung it into the middle of the kitchen table.

Pottering over in her pink, flowery apron, his mother placed the coffee cups on the table, sat down and snatched up the opened mail. She read through every word of each letter though it was obvious to Cas, from the first line, that they were rejections no matter how nice some of them sounded.

Slamming the letters down, his mother stared hard at him.

"You must be doing something wrong in the interviews, Son. You're a bright boy, but they just aren't seeing it. These ones don't even say that they'll be keeping your name on file. They're getting worse."

Ignoring her while he ripped open the last letter, he scanned it and threw it down in front of her.

"I've had interview training week in - week out and I've studied alternative techniques on the internet, Mother. I'm doing exactly what they say and I've done it that many times—I could get a job teaching it."

"Then apply for a job teaching it?"

"I don't have any qualifications to teach anything."

"What! You have piles of qualifications. All those courses the job centre sends you on are qualifications."

"They aren't. That pile of certificates is exactly that. A pile of certificates. Health and Safety, First aid, Health and Hygiene, I even got a Street-works ticket out of them which are like gold dust to get hold of, but they don't qualify me to do zilch."

"So, what's the point of them making you do them?"

"Basically, to show employers that I have more certificates than the next man or woman. It saves them having to get me through any necessary courses."

"And you have a whole stack of them, yet they still don't give you a job. It must be something to do with you personally, Son."

"I lack any experience, Mother. That is what employers want. Six months experience even for the simplest, lowest-paid job and that's where I get pipped at the post every time. There's always someone who has experience. I have none and never will have at this rate."

"Well, you need to get some."

Slamming his forehead down on the table, Cas groaned.

"Getting mad won't get you anywhere," she said.

Shaking her head at him, whilst sipping her coffee, caused his mum to miss her mouth and the hot coffee ran down her chin and into her cleavage. Jumping up out of the chair, she ran for the kitchen roll.

Cas looked up and then turned his attention away from her, as she mopped up the spill around her bra. He opened his laptop and searched his inbox for more bad news. Open-mouthed he read through an email once, twice and on the third time his mother returned to her seat and picked up her coffee again.

"What is it, Son?"

Hesitating a moment, to be certain of what he was seeing, Cas replied. "I've got a job."

Again the coffee was spilled, across the table this time and into the rejection letters, as his mother leapt from her chair and ran around the table. She read what Cas was staring at.

"What sort of job is that?"

"It's from the interview I had in Greenford about two weeks ago. It's something to do with computers and monitoring things—I think. It's a big company and looking at this, the position is available in Berrycroft. Where's Berrycroft?"

"I've never heard of it. Put it in your map thingy."

Cas typed the address into his browser. He stared and frowned at the map, as he tried to find somewhere recognisable nearby. He zoomed out and out again until he had the outline of the country on the screen.

"What! That's gotta be a hundred miles away. That's typical—the first job I get and I can't take it. Forget it!"

"Why can't you take it?"

"It'll take me all day to get there and back. The wages wouldn't even cover the travelling costs."

His mother slunk away and soaked up the spilt coffee. She took a deep breath and her face turned very serious. Cas knew some kind of lecture was probably to follow.

"What?" he asked, uncomfortable from her glaring eyes.

"You could always move there. You are nearly thirty years old, after all. You can't be hanging from my apron strings forever and it's not like there's anything keeping you here. When do they want you to start?"

Cas was shocked. He'd never considered moving out, let alone to a new town. He tried his hardest to think of reasons why it would be impossible.

"Well, what about you? You'd be all on your own here?"

"I've got Moby to keep me company. He's been here longer than you have," she said, as she sprinkled some fish food into the glass bowl on the table. Moby the immortal goldfish rose to the surface and sucked them up.

"But a fish isn't like me."

"While there is something alive in a house, you can never be lonely."

"He can't talk to you, cook for you or look after you if

you're sick."

"I'm not an old woman. I'm quite capable of looking after myself. In fact, it'll be easier on my own without a baby to keep an eye on. When are you starting the job?"

"They want me to start on Monday, but I can't find anywhere to live that quick and I don't have any money. It's a ridiculous idea, Mum."

"You've got plenty of time to find somewhere to live. You start now while you're on the internet. I'll give you the money to get moved and settled."

Cas couldn't understand his mother's eagerness to kick him from the nest. She wasn't usually a hurtful woman.

Tapping her finger on the top of his laptop she said, "Get searching," before leaving him alone. With her back to him, she washed the milk pan in the sink and hummed a happy tune.

Cas got to work at flat hunting in silence. The email that he'd waited so long for had lost its thrill. Instead, he wished it had never come or at least that he'd deleted it before his mother had seen it.

Things started looking up for him as he browsed the net for accommodation. He turned, trying his best to look defeated, to his mother.

"It's no good, Mum. Every one of them wants references from a previous landlord. It's as useless as trying to get a job without experience. I'm wasting my time."

"But you have found a job without having experience. Nothing is impossible and let that be a lesson to you, Son."

Without another word, his mother disappeared upstairs. Checking through more sites, Cas was certain she was wrong. There wasn't anything anywhere that didn't require something or other of which he hadn't got.

When she returned, she held out a bundle of twenty

pound notes.

"I suggest you get on a train to Berrycroft, check the local papers, shop windows or find a pub and ask the locals. Sometimes the old ways are still the best. How do you think we all managed before the days of the internet? There's enough money here to put you up in a bed and breakfast for the time being. I'll dig out the suitcase from the loft. Do you need anything ironing?"

Cas was flabbergasted by his mother's harsh reaction. He took the money from her hand, as it sank into his brain that she was deadly serious. Shaking his head at the ironing offer, he skulked off to his bedroom and began sorting what he thought he'd need, after his eviction, for his new life.

Joining him soon after in his room, his mother swung a very old, but hardly used, suitcase onto his bed.

"There'll be plenty of room for a week's worth of clothes in there. You'll have to find a launderette if you don't find a place with washing facilities. Don't try overloading the case with bumph you don't need. You could be carrying it for a long time. I'm sorry it doesn't have wheels, but they weren't invented when I bought it."

Looking around his room at all the possessions he'd collected over the years, his games consoles, his guitar, his CD and DVD collection, Cas tried to figure what would be most important for him to squash into his case. His mother began filling it with pants, socks, shirts and trousers while tossing aside trainers, tracksuits and hoodies.

"Stop looking at your toys. You don't need them—you're going to work. They'll all still be here when you come to visit."

"They aren't toys Mum—they're ..."

"If they aren't making you any money, then they're toys."

She shut the case and forced the zip round. Taking the biggest, thickest coat from the wardrobe, she marched out of the room. Cas lifted the case from the bed and followed her downstairs to the kitchen. Things were happening far too fast for him to get his head around. His mother had unplugged his laptop and was winding the lead up as he entered the room.

"I can do that myself, Mum."

"I'm helping, okay. You want to be getting on your way if you're going to make it before the day's out. If you get held up and have to sleep rough tonight, you've got that coat there to keep you warm. You're quite lucky you landed the job while the weather's still nice."

As Cas put his laptop into its bag, tucked his leads into the side pockets and unplugged his phone that had been on charge, he wondered if he was in some horrible nightmare. After all these years of thinking his mother enjoyed having her son living with her, she didn't seem to care two jots that he was leaving. In fact she was positively, forcibly shoving him away, pushing him and his belongings out of the door and off to the other side of the country. It might have been to the farthest place in the world in Cas's view. He tried once more to reason with her.

"Mother, I'm really not sure that this is such a good idea."

"Well, you won't know that until you get there and if you don't go, you'll never know whether it was or wasn't. I'll ring you a cab."

"I can ring the cab myself. I'm not a child anymore."

"Glad to hear it."

Cas dialled for a cab to the station. He hadn't a clue what train he needed to catch, but he wasn't going to make a big fuss about it. She was obviously in a hurry to see the back of him and if he was going to leave in a manly fashion - then he'd sort out his travel arrangements himself en route.

"It'll be here in five minutes."

"Oh, good. You can make yourself a sandwich to take with you while you wait."

Doing as he was told, he made himself a packed lunch. He couldn't get over his mother's eagerness to be rid of him. Maybe she was ill. She wasn't really old enough to be suffering from the things old people get that change their personalities, but it was very disturbing for him to think that she could be so cold about the whole thing.

The taxi beeped its horn. Cas put on his coat and carried the suitcase and his bag to the door with his mother in quick pursuit.

She hugged him on the doorstep and shed a tear. It had crossed his mind that she might have been joking all along and change her mind, but as she sniffed, he realised it was no prank and no bad dream. The taxi driver threw the case in the boot and Cas got in and closed the door. As the cab pulled away, his mother waved her hanky and closed the front door before he was even out of view.

Although the taxi driver tried to make conversation on the journey, Cas only answered with grunts and wasn't even aware what the guy was saying to him. It was only half an hour ago that he'd been sitting at the kitchen table expecting nothing out of the ordinary to occur. It was odd that in such a short space of time he'd got a job, was travelling halfway across the country to a place he'd never heard of and, to top it all, he was homeless. Berrycroft sounded like a nice place, but so did Watermeadows, the estate near the train station which they were passing through. It wasn't a nice place at all, renowned for burning cars that kept the streets lit up at night-time; even the residents had to collect their own mail from the sorting office because the postmen refused to go there for fear of being mugged or attacked. He began to imagine that Berrycroft would be the same and he'd be a stranger in this terrible place.

"Mate! We're here." The taxi driver jolted Cas from his daydream.

Cas paid and tipped the driver, who seemed oblivious to the daunting journey that he was undertaking.

Entering the train station, he searched for the screen that mentioned Berrycroft. Not finding anything, he asked at the ticket counter for instructions and was told he had to change trains three times and at which stations. The girl was really helpful and she wrote it all down for him, but the route would take him up and down the country all day to get him where he needed to be. He bought a book at the station shop. Not that he ever read books, but he needed something to bide the time. He didn't want to waste his laptop or phone battery without knowing if and when he'd be able to charge them up again. He waited at platform three breathing in the smell of burning rubber from the nearby estate and he struggled to fight the notion that Berrycroft could be worse.

Arriving at Berrycroft station in the early evening, Cas sniffed the air. There was no smell of smoke to his delight. Getting into a cab, he asked to be taken to the BEET offices - his new place of work. He realised finding a place to stay could be difficult and that the closer he started to his place of employment, the less time he'd have to travel each day. The journey was short and the taxi driver stopped outside a grim-looking building with no windows.

"That's six quid, Mate."

"Could you carry on to the nearest pub? One that has

rooms if you know of any. I'm not familiar with this area."

Well, that was Cas's first boo-boo of his new life. Even he was aware that you should never tell a taxi driver that you are unfamiliar with the area, but he'd had a long day and was pretty tired of traveling.

The taxi drove around the streets, pulling up outside of four pubs in all; all of which were boarded up.

"Sorry, Mate. There's one closing down every day. I'll find you one eventually."

He finally stopped outside The White Horse Inn. There did seem to be some signs of life, as a dim glow emanated from the frosted windows.

"That's twenty-one pounds, please."

Cas gasped, as he wondered how far they must have travelled. "How far is the BEET office from here on foot?"

"Ten-minutes' walk. It's not that far. It's just we've been going round in circles, you know?"

Cas paid the cabbie and learnt his first lesson. He needed to be on the ball a lot more.

He hauled his case into the pub and took a seat at the bar.

A pretty barmaid smiled at him.

"What can I get you?"

"Pint of lager, please. Whichever's cheapest."

"Sure. You aren't from round here by the sounds of that accent?"

"No. I'm starting a new job on Monday. I need to find myself somewhere to stay. Do you do rooms here?"

"Sorry, we don't. Even if we did, I wouldn't recommend you going up there. The Oak used to, but it closed down about six months ago. That's three twenty, please." She placed his pint on the bar and held her hand out.

"Well, do you know anywhere around here that I can

get a bed for the night?" Cas fumbled for the right change. His roll of money wasn't going to last him very long at this rate.

"Is that your best chat-up line?" The barmaid winked at him and turned to the till.

"No. I'm sorry. I didn't mean it to sound like that. I need to get somewhere permanent eventually, but temporary will do for now." His cheeks burned twice as hard as he was embarrassed by the fact that he'd blushed in the first instance.

"You know, you might be in luck. There's a fella, Yahoo his name is, he pops in most nights and I know he's got a spare room. He's just bought one of those swanky new flats where the old mill used to be. If not, there are plenty of hotels nearer to town and if worse comes to worse, I could ring my boyfriend and convince him to let you stay at his place. He'll find you and kill you if you steal anything, so be warned."

She winked again, but Cas didn't see the funny side of the comment. He could picture the scene. A big angry boyfriend kicking the shit out of him because this minx of a barmaid had hidden the guy's treasured possession on purpose. He sipped at his beer and looked around the room in an attempt to end the conversation, but she wasn't letting him off that easily.

"So what's your name, anyhow?"

"Cas. Cas Howard."

"Pleased to meet you Cas. That's easy for me to remember. I have an auntie Cassie. I'm Lexy. Well, my real name's Felicity, but all my friends call me Lexy."

Cas nodded and did his best to hold in his blushes. There was something strangely provocative about both names and he was sure the girl had undone another of her blouse buttons while she'd been at the till.

The pub door opened and Lexy held up her finger.

"Here's your man now. Perfect timing." She started pouring a beer before the guy had even reached the bar and her timing was perfect too. She placed the drink next to Cas, as the tall, smiling guy held out a fifty pound note.

"Yahoo. I'd like you to meet Cas. He's new in town and looking for a place to stay. You're looking for a flatmate, right?" She winked.

He turned to Cas and shook his hand. "You working?"

"Yes. I'm starting next Monday—at the BEET office." Cas was astounded by the speed of things and his own luck.

"You poor fella. Have a drink with me. You look clean enough. If you haven't irritated me within half an hour, then the room is yours." He ruffled Cas's hair and pushed at his head like you would a dog.

It was a friendly gesture, but one that seemed over familiar from someone Cas had only just met.

"How much is the room?"

"Ah, we'll talk money later. Now, where'd you get that accent from?"

Lexy leant over the bar to give Yahoo his change.

"I think it's a cool accent," she remarked.

Yahoo raised his eyebrows at her.

"What's with all the niceties today? Don't be fooled by her, Cas. She's an evil little witch most of the time."

Not knowing whether to smile at the banter or look shocked at the insult, Cas lifted his pint to his lips to hide any expression. It seemed to him that Yahoo was either young for his confidence or was much older and looked good for his age. His face wasn't symmetrical, but it was quite good-looking for a guy. The dark hair and square sideburns looked groomed, but natural at the same time. The fact that he'd paid for a pint with a fifty pound note eased Cas's fears that the man might rob him in his sleep.

Before Cas could answer the question about his accent, which seemed to have been forgotten anyway, an influx of people distracted Lexy's attention from him and Yahoo was greeted with handshakes like he's someone famous.

An excited-looking man tapped Cas on the shoulder.

"Are you joining in the quiz tonight?"

"Um ... I don't know. Will he be doing it?" Cas replied, nodding towards Yahoo.

"If he's drinking beer, he will be. If he's drinking orange, he'll be shooting off."

"He's drinking beer."

"Then he's in. What about you?"

"Yes. I'm in."

"That's two quid then. Are you paying for him as well?"

"I guess so." Cas handed him a fiver.

Lexy shouted over, "I'm in their team."

"That's another quid then, Mate."

Cas gave him another pound and received a pen and a sheet of paper. Although his mother had given him a large wad of money, he knew he wouldn't be paid until the end of the month and he'd have to curb spending it at the rate he was.

The quizmaster left him and went off to harass other people. Finished with his pats on the back, Yahoo turned back to Cas.

"Oh, shit. I forgot it was Friday. Has he roped us in to his dodgy quiz?"

"Sorry! He said you'd be doing it."

"He didn't say we'd win though. That table over there always wins. It must be a fix. I can't see how, if they are that clever, why they haven't got jobs. Not one of them works."

"Maybe they study all day."

"Maybe they do. Boring old farts they are. I like your thinking. Another beer?"

"Yeah! Go on then." Cas knew he was going to get on with this guy. He'd never met anyone so laid back, yet so confident in himself.

The quiz turned out to be more fun than Cas had expected. Between the three of them they made up the most ridiculous answers to the questions that they didn't know. Yahoo had a knack for reading into the questions in an obscure way and whilst his answers made sense to his own interpretation, they weren't literally correct and didn't amuse the brainy table that were marking his sheet. Even when Cas knew the right answer, he went with the one Yahoo had suggested. He could see the three of them were having a much better time than the stuffy people on the winning table and he understood that trying to win was pointless.

"It's wasted on them." Yahoo said extremely loudly after every round.

When the table were handed a hundred pounds at the end of the quiz, Cas slightly regretted not taking it more seriously. Only slightly, though.

The two of them drank into the early hours of the morning. There was no regard for the licensing laws in the place. While they still had a small amount of sense and balance left, they said their goodbyes to the real night owls and struggled off up the street taking it in turns to fall onto and over the suitcase.

Reaching the flat, Cas had lost all focus in his eyesight. The door, walls, floor and ceiling spun around him and it was only Yahoo's arm that kept him on his feet and moving forwards.

"That's your room," Yahoo said, pushing him through a

door. Cas entered, stumbled and crashed onto the bed. Literally.

Yahoo

Cas woke early with a stonking headache. At first, he wondered where he was, as he looked around the plain but spotless modern room. He realised there'd be no mother appearing to scold him for being lazy, so he buried his head below the duvet and went back to sleep for some hours.

Later, he was awoken by knocking and Yahoo's concerned voice.

"Are you okay, Cas?"

"Yes. I'm barely alive, but I'm still here."

"Great. Can I come in? I've got some towels for the en suite. I didn't know if you brought one with you."

"Yeah sure, come in. En suite?"

Yahoo entered the room and placed two brown towels on the bed. "Yeah, through there's your own toilet and shower."

Cas sat up rubbing at his face and scratching through his hair. He'd never seen brown towels before. His mother always bought pale blue ones to match the bathroom décor. These were definitely man towels.

"I feel like shit, Man. My own loo you say—this place is great. I'm gonna need it though—right now. You'd better get out of here."

Not needing a warning, Yahoo was out of the room.

"I'll make you a banana and egg smoothy. It'll make

you normal again."

With his hand on his stomach, Cas felt it somersault.

"I'd rather have a coffee," he yelled after him. Hearing the blender fire up, he guessed he hadn't heard.

Emptied, showered and dressed, Cas joined Yahoo in the kitchen and they sipped at their slimy drinks.

"That shower nearly hammered me through the floor." Cas laughed.

"You can turn the power down. You'll get used to the place. Just make yourself at home. I'm usually working in the office, through there, but I'm starting late today."

"Won't they mind?"

Yahoo laughed. "No! I had a word with the boss this morning. He said I'm brilliant and can do whatever I like whenever I like."

"Really?" Cas thought this was awesome.

"Of course. I work for myself, Cas. It does wonders for my ego."

Feeling slightly foolish, Cas forced a feeble chuckle. "What is it you do?"

"This and that, computer stuff, things other people can't do for themselves. Adverts, websites and all that boring, time-consuming nonsense that no one else wants to waste their time on. You'd be amazed at how many people can't change a simple doc to a Pdf. There's no point explaining it to them. I get sent lists of things to do and tell them it'll take a couple of days. They're more than happy to throw their money around to save them the stress. They make me laugh. 'Save them the stress'—it's a ten-minute job for me."

"Sounds like easy money, but not that much fun. I guess being your own boss is pretty cool, though."

"Oh, I have plenty of fun. It's not all office work. That's just the steady income part of it. I hang onto it in case my luck runs out or I lose my gift."

Cas realised Yahoo had a way about himself that created intrigue. The more he was telling him the less Cas knew, but it drew him in and he could see why so many people had flocked around Yahoo last night at the bar, as if he was some kind of celebrity. He was the kind of guy that you'd never get bored of being with.

Cas had to ask. "Your gift? What would that be I wonder?"

"Ha! You are very astute. It's no secret though. It's the gift of being in the right place at the right time. You could call it luck, but sometimes I sense it and I have to follow it."

Now Cas was more cautious, as he sensed a hint of bullshit. He was unsure if Yahoo was being serious or merely creating a mystical image of himself.

"You're good at the talk, Yahoo, but what are you getting at? I'm not a psychic."

"You must have seen some of my videos—at least some of those that went viral. I haven't met a person yet who hasn't. Come with me."

Cas followed him through to the office room which Yahoo had pointed out earlier. He stared around in wonderment at all the technical equipment. He could see what his mother had meant now by 'his toys'. This was real hi-tech stuff and not a games console in sight.

"This must have cost you a fortune."

"It paid for itself. No worries. Brand new car, newly built flat, everything I own has all come from computers, technology and my luck. The only test I've ever taken was my driving test. I didn't pass that until I was thirty years old and that was only because I had to, after I'd bought the car. I'm not qualified in anything."

So without asking the age question, Cas had some idea

that Yahoo was not much older than him. He'd check the reg of the car and work it out at some point. He didn't like asking personal questions. There was one that he had to ask though, as he already thought he'd figured it out.

"I take it your name isn't really Yahoo? Is it a nickname you got from your computer work?"

"It's a nickname alright, but no relation to computers. It doesn't really help at all. You'd have a hard job finding me if you type Yahoo into any computer. Luckily, my fans know that and subscribe to my sites. This video will explain why the name Yahoo. You might have seen it before. It's been knocking around for a while now."

Yahoo clicked on one of the laptops and typed something in. A video popped open and Cas watched with a vague recollection of seeing it before.

He recognised it was Yahoo standing at a bar. Rodeo music began playing in the background and another guy brought over a bar stool and placed it next to Yahoo. He nodded a thank you and pushed up an imaginary hat with his finger before pointing into the air and miming the firing of guns which had been added to the soundtrack. He then sat on the stool wrapping his feet around its legs. He gripped the front of the stool with one hand and waved the other in the air. He rocked back and forth, gently at first, swinging the stool onto the two front legs and back onto the two back legs over and over while keeping his centre of gravity perfect so as not to tip the stool completely. With a jerk from his body, the stool began to run like a bucking horse across the floor of the bar while its rider yelled out, "Yahoo." Someone opened the front door and the angry barstool continued into the street. Whoever was filming it, followed him outside as he continued howling Yahoo and the film ended as he rounded a corner out of view.

Cas was laughing hysterically. Although he'd seen it before and found it funny, it was even funnier standing next to the star of the video.

"So that's why they call you Yahoo, right?"

"Right! And that video was also the start of my viral career. That's what started the money pouring in and it hasn't stopped coming."

"But surely the shot belonged to the guy that was filming it."

"Nope. It was all set up. I know it looks like a silly drunken scene in a pub, shot in one take, but it wasn't. I gave a mate my phone to film it. We had about two hours of video that I edited to make that short scene. Do you know how hard barstool riding is? I'd never have got that far in one go."

"You've spoilt it for me now. It doesn't look set up at all. Do you set them all up?"

"Not at all. I do have a knack of being in the right place, like I said, and I get a sense that something's going to happen. My advice is—make sure your phone or camera is always on and ready to shoot. The best things are often over in a flash and even if you catch them, without the build-up you lose the anticipation. The important part is always the editing though. The timing has to be spot on. That's the difference between a funny video and one that'll go viral."

Cas had lost all his qualms about Yahoo; he was now in awe of the guy. To make so much money in such a fun way had to be every guy's dream job.

"How many videos have you made?"

"Who knows? Hundreds of single ones, compilations and I redo and resurrect ones that didn't take off the first time. Even stills make money if you can add a smart caption. I was going to edit this one that I shot last night, but I think I'll hang onto it for a while in case I ever have to blackmail you."

Cas frowned and wondered what he meant; he'd been with him all last night and didn't recall seeing him filming anything.

Yahoo tapped the laptop and a new video appeared. It was a close-up shot of Cas's terribly drunken-looking face. The barmaid could be seen and only just heard in the background. "Goodnight guys. Be careful on your way home."

Watching in horror as his wobbling eyes tried to focus on her, Cas heard himself call out, "I'd take you with me if you didn't have a big fuck-ugly boyfriend that would kill me."

Yahoo was laughing and started it up again.

Cas stared open-mouthed, as he watched it a second time. He stood silent for a few seconds before responding.

"Shit! I don't remember saying that. If her boyfriend sees that he will kill me. You can't put that out there."

"You were pretty smashed. I wanted to take a shot of the state of you leaving the pub and show you it today. Nothing more than to tease you about that face. I was as surprised as you are when you came out with that line. Don't worry. I won't post it anywhere. I'm just showing you how simple it is and you didn't even notice I was filming you. There's not that much to edit—just a bit of work on the sound quality. I might use it one day."

He winked at Cas who was still in shock and not by the video, but by his own words.

"I would never dream of saying something like that to a girl normally. That is awful. What if she tells her boyfriend what I said?"

"Lexy! I wouldn't worry about her. She puts up with far worse shit than that. I'd say she forgot about it the minute you were out the door. Don't worry about her and don't apologise to her whatever you do—she'll have you round her finger if she thinks you're weak. Pretend you can't remember."

"I can't remember. If you hadn't shown me that, I'd be none the wiser. I'm gonna be so embarrassed next time I go in the pub."

"Forget it happened—put it out of your mind. Anyhow, I have work to do, so shift. Why don't you have a walk about and find your way around the place, and remember to have your phone at the ready."

"Yeah, I will. I could do with some fresh air. I'll see you later."

Wandering for five minutes, the fresh air only made him feel sick. He went back to the flat and, not disturbing Yahoo, he went back to bed where he stayed. Yahoo didn't disturb him either.

Cas was awoken the following morning by the sound of banging and clattering around. He couldn't believe his head was still sore after so much sleep. He vowed never ever to drink so much again. Two pints at any one time would have to be his limit. Work was the most important thing right now and time off with a hangover wasn't going to pay his rent.

Hearing the flat door slam and echo around his head, he got up and went through to the kitchen in search of coffee. There was a note scrawled on a piece of paper next to the kettle. 'I have a mission. Have a nice day. Yahoo.'

Unsure of what it meant, but clear that Yahoo wouldn't be returning, Cas found the coffee and called his mother. Usually on a Sunday, he'd already be dicing carrots. She didn't have time to chat with him, though; she said she was preparing dinner.

Setting up his laptop, he decided to subscribe to some

of Yahoo's sites and he was surprised by how quickly the day passed watching the funny videos. A surge of ravenous hunger hit him late afternoon, so he called for a pizza delivery and munched through it while watching the more serious news reports that Yahoo had shot the footage for. Thinking back over his own lifespan, he could only recall four or five incidences where he had seen something worthy of videoing, had he been ready with camera. It was unbelievable to think that one guy, Yahoo, could have found himself in the right spot time after time to have such a vast catalogue of material. He had said that he had a gift and Cas recognised that that was clearly what he had.

His mind became nervous about his new job, so he had a shower and laid out his clothes for work. He set the alarm on his mobile and put on a film. It crossed his mind to pop to the pub and apologise to Lexy, but he recalled what Yahoo had told him and decided it wasn't a good idea to be drinking the night before his first day in his first ever job. Yahoo still hadn't returned by the time he went to bed. It was one of the most unfulfilling days he'd ever had. No mail, no rejections, no Sunday dinner to roast, but tomorrow he'd be working and although he was nervous, the excitement of real work, job satisfaction and a wage overruled his anxiety.

Work

Waking before his alarm had gone off, Cas was back to his usual self again. It had only taken him a whole weekend to get over his hangover, which may sound far-fetched, but he was not a seasoned drinker.

Greeting him in the kitchen with a big smile on his face, Yahoo offered to make him a coffee.

"Are you nervous?" he asked.

"A little, but I'm really looking forward to it. The nerves are self-doubt—I think I'll mess up or break something and get sacked. I know it's ridiculous, but it's my kind of luck."

Yahoo rubbed his shoulder against him.

"You'll be fine, Mate. There's some Yahoo luck rubbing off on you—I can feel it. I had a great day yesterday. This band called me to film their video. They didn't want it to look like a real shoot, more like a fan had caught the footage while they were practising. They weren't even playing or singing live—they just wanted it to come across like they were. It's the first time I've been asked to do something like that and although I could see their thinking behind it, it's a bit of a dumb thing to do. Anyone who does go to see them live is gonna be very disappointed cos they are pretty crap. Don't get me wrong the studio technician did a brilliant job with their track, but they have no way of emulating it live. I don't care. They've paid me for the video and I have some great footage of the fight they had before and after. It'll pay well if they ever get famous. The guitarist punched the female drummer straight in the face. It looks a shocking thing to do, but the girl got up and pummelled the guy to near unconsciousness. You should have seen the muscles on her."

"It sounds fantastic, but I have to go," Cas said.

"I've got a scooter in the garage if you want to borrow it. It's old, but it was my first taste of freedom and I've hung on to it for sentimental reasons and to remind of the days before the flash car—when it was only a dream."

"Thanks, but it's only a ten-minute walk. I'll leave it for today."

The offer gave him a sense of satisfaction. He knew Yahoo trusted him and saw him as a friend.

"Good luck. Oops. Break a leg," Yahoo yelled after him, as he left the flat.

The street was busy with people rushing or strolling to work. Cas was in no hurry, but he was too exhilarated to stroll, so he walked awkwardly and consciously as if everyone around him knew it was his first day of his first ever job. In reality, he merged in fine and was ignored by all.

Entering the BEET office building he stopped and stood tall, like a real man, for the first time in his life. Then he called his mother to tell her that he'd arrived on time.

She congratulated him and wished him luck.

At reception a security man told him to wait for someone to collect him, so instead of sitting down, he wandered around reading the notices on the wall. He was aware of the cameras in every corner and thought it would make him look enthusiastic and interested in the company.

He was greeted by a large, stern-looking man, but as he spoke Cas realised the guy's tongue was actually bigger than the greedy mouth it was squeezed into. Drops of spit spattered Cas's face, and like the fool he was, Cas was too afraid to brush them away for fear of seeming rude. He imagined the foreign germs breeding rapidly on his warm pink cheek. He nodded repeatedly hoping the man would stop talking and give him the chance to decontaminate himself. Finally, he did stop, though Cas was totally unaware of what he'd agreed to or confirmed.

The pair walked into a kind of airlock door where the boss man chuckled and spat again in Cas's face.

"Bendy Wendy will be training you." Forcing himself to stop chuckling, by putting his hand over his mouth and coughing, the man opened the second door and they entered into a very large, noisy room. It was sparse of people and there were five times as many empty workstations as manned ones. Not one eye looked up as they passed down a row of busy, pale people.

"You can sit here. I'll let Wendy know you're waiting. Fire it up while you wait." The man left him sitting there. Cas switched on the computer and the screen lit up and asked for his password. Not having a password, Cas twiddled his thumbs for about twenty minutes while all around him phones rang and people swore and growled.

A fortyish-year-old woman came frolicking towards him with a big smile.

"Hello! You must be Cas. I'm Wendy. Do you smoke?"

"Hello, Wendy. Um … no. I don't smoke."

"Well, pretend you do. Come with me and I'll show you where the smoking area and the fire drill points are. Turn that off first. Always turn off your workstation before you leave it, even if it's only for a wee-wee. You could get into serious trouble if someone interfered while you're logged in."

"I'm not logged in yet. I don't have a password."

"Don't worry. We'll get the tech guy to sort that out later."

He followed the wiggling woman, who swished her hair constantly with a flick of the head as she passed the rows of wired-up workers. They went through the airlock and out of the building. She immediately lit up a cigarette.

"Are you sure you don't want one?" she asked, holding out the packet.

"No. Really, I don't smoke."

"Well, if you ever start, this is the smoking area. You have to ask permission from the team leader if you want to leave your workstation."

"Who's the team leader?"

Wendy started walking and twitched her head for Cas to follow her.

"There are different team leaders. I think it's James today. The teams work shifts, so you'll meet them all, as you're on days for now. You'll get to know them all and their different ways of doing things. Round here is the fire assembly point. If the alarm goes off, everyone meets up here. Saying that—the alarms are always going off in there. We test them twice a day and it only takes an impatient employee to try and open the airlock door before the click and an alarm will go off. Just ignore them. There's never been a fire yet."

She lit up another cigarette.

"When I started here, I was doing what you're doing. I wept in the toilets every chance I could get. It was so daunting and I didn't think I'd ever understand what was going on, so don't be ashamed if you feel the need for a little cry. My desk is on the end of the front row if you need any consolation."

Cas couldn't imagine how bad a job could be that it would make anyone cry. He got the impression this woman wanted to be needed far more than he'd want to be consoled by her.

"What is it exactly that we do here? I've read some of the information, but it doesn't seem to tell me anything significant."

"Don't worry. The training will make all that clear to you. You have a lovely accent and a clear voice. That'll go well for you on the phones."

Two more cigarettes and some chitchat about her wasted life and Wendy headed back to the door. Cas followed in silence. His questions weren't being answered, so he'd given up asking them.

Back in the airlock, she clapped her hands together.

"We'd better get you some training done then. Do you want coffee or would you like one of my special hot chocolates with mini marsh mallows?"

"Coffee will be fine, thanks. Milk, six sugars, but don't stir it cos it makes it too sweet." Cas waited for a reaction from the little wisecrack that his mother always used, but it didn't go as expected.

The door clicked and Wendy opened it wide. "After you, Sweet-tooth."

Sitting back at his workstation with a screen that read only 'enter password', Cas watched the welfare-room door where Wendy had disappeared through to make coffee. Each time someone entered or left, he caught a glimpse of her chatting, laughing and flicking her hair. Thinking he might have been forgotten about, he looked around at the other members of staff and tried to catch their eye. They all looked so busy, but eventually a girl threw her hands in the air and rolled her eyes. Doing so, she spotted Cas staring at her and glared back mouthing the word 'What?'

He pointed at his screen and shrugged his shoulders. She copied his action before pointing at her headset, speaking into the mouthpiece and getting back to work.

Two cups, one of coffee and one of froth with pasty lumps floating on top appeared on the desk. Wendy leant over Cas's shoulder and tapped her own password into his keyboard. Then she began the training. Cas tried his best to pick up everything she was showing and telling him. The confusing mess on the screen was hard enough for him to understand, but her use of acronyms, which he had no idea of the meaning of, made her sound like she was speaking in a foreign language.

It didn't help his concentration that she didn't take a seat. Instead she leant over him with her bust at his eye-level and her blouse gaping open giving him an eyeful of her right breast. Thankfully, she was wearing a bra, but the way the bosom swung as she tapped at the keyboard, it could have popped out at any moment.

Cas tried his hardest to stop his eyes flicking from the screen to the bosom. A creepy thought entered his head that she was doing it on purpose, but he dismissed it. She was surely too old and professional to act in that way.

Pausing from her relentless spiel, she held out a sheet of paper to him.

"This is what you say when you answer the telephone. It might look like a lot to learn, but you'll do it automatically in no time. Now you'll hear my sexy phone voice."

Putting the headset on, she clicked a button on the phone and within a second it rang. Another tap and she was talking to whoever was on the other end. Her voice had definitely changed. It was younger, deeper, flirtier and provocatively sexy.

Flicking through pages on the screen, that Cas didn't recall seeing during his training, she did all kinds of actions and text typing while discussing what the weather was like where the caller was.

"Thank you, too. Goodbye ... I love you too."

Flummoxed by the last part of the phone conversation, Cas wondered what kind of job he'd got himself into.

Wendy explained, "Don't worry about that one. I used to work with the guy in another branch. He's such a laugh."

She did something else on his keyboard, that he didn't understand or recognise, before removing the headset and switching off the phone.

"Have you got all that now?" she asked him, still using the sexy phone voice.

"I think so." Cas lied, but he was now uneasy at the closeness of the woman.

She handed him a pile of papers containing lists with tick boxes down the side.

"Good. Now, tick all the boxes and sign at the bottom of each sheet."

"What are they for?"

"They're just to confirm that we've been over everything and to prove you've had your training. The last one is a health and safety form. Make sure you read through it thoroughly before signing it."

Leaving him with them, she picked up her foam-filled cup and wiggled her arse back to the welfare-room. Cas did as he'd been told, still totally unaware of what his job actually entailed, ticking each box at the end of a line of illegible text and words consisting of capital letters. Reading through the final page, he checked his surroundings again. The Health and Safety form told him he must wear a hardhat when plant machinery was on site and various other strange instructions and rules that didn't fit with the office setting at all. Not questioning it, and having no one to question it with, he ticked and signed everything. So long as he did as he was told, he guessed nothing could go wrong.

Returning half an hour later, Wendy invited him out for another cigarette while the tech guy set up his password and the files he'd need to get into.

The break turned into a long hour of her chain smoking and telling him about her divorce and the shenanigans she got up to now that she was single.

All Cas could do was listen and smile, as if he was finding her company and her tales highly amusing. He was sure his headache would return if he didn't get away from the woman. Eventually she glanced at her watch and acted shocked.

"We'd better get you back inside. I'm sure the tech guy will have done everything by now."

Cas was relieved to get back to his workstation. He put on his headset, logged in, switched on the phone and was transported into a world of chaos and confusion where he spent the rest of the day completely bewildered and alone.

Leaving the office, he was no wiser as to what his job was than he had been before entering that morning.

Arriving home, he found Yahoo in the kitchen cooking.

"That looks and smells good," Cas said, leaning over a pan of meatballs in Bolognese sauce.

"Well, I saw you'd ordered a rotten takeaway pizza yesterday. You didn't even hide the box. How can you eat those things—I'd rather eat the cardboard. So, I thought I'd play Wifey, as you've been hard at work all day, and cook you up some real food." Yahoo did a twirl flashing his apron with a design of a woman's body in sexy underwear.

"Don't you start. That's the last thing I want to see right now. I've had this woman's boob on my shoulder most of the day. I swear she was coming on to me."

"Lucky you! Was she nice?"

"Don't! She's gotta be fifty years old. She looks good for it mind, but way too old for me."

Yahoo snapped a fistful of spaghetti in half and dropped it in another pan.

"You made a good impression on your first day then? I've heard you have to be mad to work in the BEET office and if you aren't mad when you go in, you are by the time you leave. How was it really?"

"Ridiculous. Honestly, I had my training and was none the wiser about what the place does or what my part in it is. When I was left to it, I answered the phone and told the people on the other end that I didn't know how to help them and to try again later."

"Seriously? And you got away with that all day?"

"All afternoon. No one came near me, so it's all I could do. I tried to figure out what their systems were about and how I could use them, but the phone rang continuously, so I just kept picking it up and telling them the same thing."

"It sounds like a great job. Ring … hello … how the hell should I know? I only work here. Bye."

Cas frowned. "I don't speak like that—do I?"

"Oh, chill out. I'm still practising your accent."

"I'd lose the apron too. You sound all camp with it on."

"It's all in your mind, Luvvie. There's a party on at the pub tonight for their football team. Something's bound to happen—I can sense it. So, if you fancy it, go and get showered and changed. This'll be another twenty minutes before it's ready."

"I would like to see if your super-senses are correct, but I'm not going on another session with you. Not after the last time and I still haven't faced Lexy since I was so rude to her." Cas made his way to his room.

While he showered, the intrigue of seeing Yahoo's sense in action got the better of him. Could this louder than life guy really have superpowers that could put him in the right place at the right time? He knew it was a silly idea, but he'd watched the evidence for himself. Yahoo had captured more than his fair share of amazing incidences in the last couple of years to last most people a life time. Setting his phone to go straight to video, Cas dressed and went through for his dinner. Surely, if Yahoo could make a living from his videos, then so could he. All he needed to do was stick around the guy and learn how he spots a potential incident. Maybe his luck really would rub off on him.

Sitting down to eat his meal, Cas held up his thumb.

"This looks delicious and yes, I will come down the pub for a couple. No more than two though. I'm not cut out for drinking and work is difficult enough without having a rotten hangover on top."

"Good one. You work in a damn office—you need to have a life and a bit of fun. You'll turn into a chicken otherwise."

It took Cas a few seconds to work out what he meant, but he remembered the pale faces of the workers and the girl that had glared at him with her hands in the air, before going straight back into the next phone call. They were like battery hens, trapped in their little pens, clucking away to produce something that Cas was not aware of yet. He'd started the day on a high as a man and in one sentence Yahoo had reduced him to a chicken, and not a very productive one. He felt better as watched Yahoo lick his plate clean. At least he had table manners if not much else.

As they walked down the road, Yahoo reminded Cas what not to do.

"You walk in there and act normal. You don't remember anything that you said on Friday night, okay? I don't want to spend the evening with her winding you up about how upset it made her and you grovelling on your knees. Act like nothing happened and I bet you—she won't even mention it."

"I will. I have forgotten it. I won't even blush—I promise, but if she does mention it, I will have to apologise."

"That's fair enough, but only if she mentions it and I assure you she won't."

They arrived at The White Horse to find a crowd of rowdy lads already half-cut and dressed as Umpa Lumpas. Apart from the slight difference in stature they were virtually identical in their dungaree shorts, green wigs and bright orange face paint.

Yahoo nudged Cas with his elbow.

"Perfect. Just perfect. Even I wasn't expecting this." He ordered the beer and the two of them sat at the bar, phones at the ready. Cas couldn't take his eyes off the group. Scanning across them to give the impression that he was just looking around, he was waiting for anyone of them to do something crazy, so he could snatch up his phone and capture the moment. He obviously wasn't as discreet as he thought.

Lexy reached over the bar and tapped his hand.

"They aren't real Umpa Lumpas—you know. And if they were, don't you know it's rude to stare?"

"Sorry. It's just funny—that's all," Cas replied, shifting his gaze to the barmaid.

She nodded. "I hope they stay funny too. These things often get messy. How did your first day at work go? It was today, wasn't it? I haven't seen you since you fell out the door with your suitcase. Yahoo said you've been ill."

"I'm fine now. I think I picked up a bug on the train on my way down. You know, not being from around here, I'm more susceptible to your germs. Work went okay, thanks. I'm a fast learner, so no problems there." Cas was sure he saw Yahoo wink, but it was difficult to tell, as he was trying hard to address Lexy while keeping the Umpa Lumpas in his peripheral vision. He didn't even notice the filthy look she gave him when he'd said 'your germs'.

"So, they might be promoting you soon?" Lexy continued with a cheeky smile.

"It's very possible once they realise what I'm capable of."

"Not if you go into work with shirts like that they won't. Did Yahoo not show you where the iron was?" She tipped her head to indicate where the worst creases were and walked away to serve an Umpa Lumpa another round of drinks.

Yahoo was chuckling. "She's good alright?"

"Is my shirt that bad? I hung it up as soon as I got it out of the suitcase and it was ironed before it went in. I didn't think it needed another ironing."

"It's not that bad. She's winding you up. I think she likes you." Yahoo winked for sure that time.

"Hmm. I seem to be getting a lot of unwanted female attention since I've been here."

"It's the accent, Mate—and what do you mean unwanted? You're not … well you know … gay are you?"

"No! I'm not gay. I meant the old nympho at work and the deadly boyfriend barmaid, Lexy. I don't have a problem with women in general. It's just typical that the ones I don't want the attention from are the ones that give me it."

"So have you got a girlfriend back home?"

"No, but I've tried a few. A fair few."

Yahoo laughed out loud. "What's that supposed to mean? I've tried a few. You make them sound like curries. Didn't you like the taste? Were they too hot for you?"

"No! Give me a break. I mean I've dated a few, but they all had kids and I didn't feel I was ready to be a dad. A few dates and the odd one-night stand is as far as I've got. One girl, same age as me, had a son who was bigger than me. It's just not something I think I'm ready for."

"Hey, I understand, Mate. It's pretty much the same for me—only I'm worried they'll try and take me for a ride and half my money. Also, my life has me shooting off here and there on the spur of the moment and there aren't many girls that will put up with that. I can't think how many dates I've missed because I've been caught up with something going off. They never believe my excuses even though I've had the evidence on my mobile. Maybe one day I'll find someone that understands my work is serious, but I'm not wasting time looking. I might just wait until I retire and create a little harem and enjoy my old age. At the moment, I like it the way it is."

Strangely Cas knew he was joking, but he could also see that it was probably the way things would pan out for Yahoo. He was the type of guy you could imagine having his own harem; it wasn't as ridiculous as it sounded. He bought the next round of drinks and watched as the Umpa Lumpas drank a round of shots in less than the time it took him to order and pay for his own.

The volume got louder with each round the team drank. Cas wondered how these so-called sportsmen could abuse their bodies with the amount of alcohol they were pushing into them and yet still function as athletes. It hadn't seemed to affect their physiques and the trophies on the shelf behind them spoke for themselves.

The singing began. Dancing on the tables, the footballers threw drinks at each other and whipped stools from under those that hadn't made the table, sending them crashing to the floor. It looked a hilarious sight, but was an uncomfortable room to be in with only the little Lexy to keep order.

Cas watched and waited for Yahoo to start filming, but he didn't. He seemed quite oblivious to the chaos and sipped his beer as if the hooligans weren't there at all.

Unable to see how the funny stuff was going to happen, all Cas could envisage was a fight breaking out and him getting his head kicked in by fifteen Umpa Lumpas. Maybe that was Yahoo's plan. It would make a great video. He could see the title. 'Chicken man gets beaten up by Umpa Lumpas.'

"I'm going for a pee and then home, Mate. I don't want to go to work with a black-eye and that's all I can see coming very soon."

"Patience is the key. Come on stay for one more."

Cas shook his head while finishing his pint and headed for the gents. As he leaned into the door, an Umpa Lumpa on the other side pulled at it to exit. Cas fell against his chest and looked up at the coke-filled nostrils. The orange head groaned and a torrent of puke sprayed out of its mouth into Cas's face and soaked into his shirt. Luckily, it didn't smell of sick and wasn't lumpy. It was purely the liquids that had recently entered the Umpa Lumpa's stomach, but the sight and thought of the puke, now cooling next to his skin, made Cas retch. He pushed past the dazed creature and ran into the cubicle. The first thought that crossed his mind was that Yahoo had filmed it. Surely he wouldn't have had a good view from where he was sitting at the bar and even if he had, he was his friend; he wouldn't humiliate him by putting it out for the whole world to see or would he? He was a businessman after all.

Cas sat on the toilet for a while to compose himself. He managed to hold his own beer inside his stomach. He was wet, but grateful that the Umpa Lumpa hadn't eaten anything before his binge drinking session.

After emptying his bladder, he left the cubicle and rinsed his face and hair in the sink. He flipped the hand dryer to face dryer and let the hot air blow across his head. He would walk straight out of the pub and hopefully no one would be any the wiser about his mishap.

Exiting the gents, the bar was oddly quiet with no signs of Umpa Lumpas. Lexy was clearing the mess they'd left behind and Yahoo was laughing at something on his phone. Cas cringed at the thought that it could be a video of him being puked on. He thought it better not to mention it in case he was wrong. He didn't want to make a laughing stock of himself.

"I'll see you later or tomorrow." Cas passed through the bar at speed, so no one would notice his wet shirt.

Yahoo looked up from his phone. "I can't believe you missed it. Where'd you go? It's a classic. I'll show you tomorrow when I've edited it."

With a wave of his hand, Cas was out the door. He'd got away with it. If Yahoo was asking him where he was, then the video was obviously not of him. He couldn't imagine what had happened in such a brief time that had caused Yahoo to be so impressed with himself.

That night Cas dreamt of the BEET office and every member of staff was an Umpa Lumpa. He awoke with a sweat on, but at least no hangover.

Wendy

His second day in the BEET office was spent as unenlightened as his first. He did get an email from the team leader who he believed was a woman sitting on the row behind him. It would have been more helpful if she'd actually come over and spoken to him, but he realised the hassle it would cause her having to log out and log in again.

He read the email. 'Your calls answered and time spent stats are excellent. Your phep stats are lower than acceptable. Make sure to pick up pheps while on calls.'

He wondered whether to reply and explain that he didn't know what a phep was. He'd signed all the paperwork stating he'd had all of his training, so they might think him thick and sack him. He ignored the email choosing to find out for himself what a phep was. Clicking through the pages and files on his computer, in search of the elusive acronym, he continued to answer the phone and inform the caller to try again later.

He wasn't offered a marshmallow hot chocolate today or any more help from Wendy. Another new member of staff had the pleasure of Wendy's tit on his shoulder on the next workstation. This time Cas had a view of her bent-over arse wiggling from side to side almost rubbing against his left shoulder. He did his best to ignore it.

It was a long day, but he got through it without doing anything that he saw as productive. He left the office with no feeling of work satisfaction, but at least he was earning his own money for the first time in his life and it made him feel a little bit more of a man.

On his walk home, he called his mother and told her about the email praising him for his excellent stats. Her proud applause brought shame on him. He was fooling his mum and he knew she could always tell when he was hiding something. He tried not to think about his conflicting personality of man versus naughty boy and remembered that he had a treat back at the flat. He quickened his step at the excitement of Yahoo revealing what he'd missed the night before.

The flat smelt good again, but exactly the same as it had done yesterday. Yahoo was wearing his sexy apron and pulled a huge lasagne from the oven.

"Magnifico."

Cas smiled. "You really don't have to cook every night. I don't mind taking my turn. My job isn't so hard that I'm incapable of doing my bit around here."

"Cas, I love cooking. I never bothered when I was on my own. I lived on soup and toast. It's not the same cooking for yourself. It's my pleasure, honestly. If you want to do your bit, you can clean the toilets and the showers. I hate that job."

"I should have kept my mouth shut. Did you edit your video?"

"I did. It's out there already, but wait 'til after dinner. Be patient—you can't eat garlic bread cold."

They ate in silence and Cas was impressed by the lasagne. He had tried making it on one occasion to surprise his mother, but it came out hard and was like chewing on leather. His mother had refused to eat it and told him to stick to what she'd taught him and what she liked eating. Foreign stuff was not her idea of a decent wholesome meal. He'd never tried making anything exotic again. This lasagne was soft and delicious. It flicked though Cas's mind to get the recipe and take it home with him. Maybe if he got it right, his mother would give it another try and be impressed by it. A second later he realised he wasn't ever going home. He had flown the nest. A pang of homesickness hit him for the first time.

After licking his plate, Yahoo stood up and without saying a word, patted Cas on the shoulder before loading up the dish washer.

Cas wondered whether Yahoo really did have a sixth sense for things or whether he himself was so transparent that it was clear that he'd just had a moment of melancholy. The little pat was comforting and lifted his spirit.

"Let's see it then—the video."

"I'll have to tell you what you missed first."

The two of them walked through to Yahoo's office as he recounted the incident.

"As soon as you went for a pee, this huge black woman dressed in a long choir robe walked in and straight over to the footballers. At first, I thought it was one of their mothers and I was expecting her to give them a good telling off. When she began singing, I knew that someone, or one of them, must have ordered a strip-o-gram. They were so far gone on drink and charlie, and whatever else they'd taken, that as soon as she whipped off her cassock, or whatever it's called, they started hurling abuse at her. Horrid racist and fat abuse. Well, I wasn't going to make a video of that. It wasn't at all funny and I felt sorry for the woman. Then she picked up a glass and threw it at them. It hit one of them straight on the forehead. That's when I left. I went over the street and stood on the corner. Then this happened."

Yahoo clicked on the play button. The scene was the front of the pub and a silly soundtrack faded in.

One after another the fifteen Umpa Lumpas streamed out of the pub and ran up the hill holding onto their wigs. The last one was followed by a flying stool before the huge figure in gold sequined knickers, that were barely visible with two tassels swinging from her nipples, launched herself out into the street. Not even attempting to cover her assets, she ran like an athlete up the road after her offenders. The shot followed them out of view and then panned back to the pub. Yahoo walked towards the door and could be heard saying, "This looks like my kind of pub." The video stopped.

Cas stood open-mouthed. The video was side-splittingly funny, but he couldn't believe what had happened in the time it took him to wash and dry his hair.

Yahoo clicked the play button again and, less interested in the funny situation, he explained his way through it.

"You see the perfect amount of timing I've used for the shot of the pub to build the anticipation. Look here at their shadows as they run up the street. The sun was low—just before setting. The long shadows actually make the footballers bodies look much smaller than they really are. The stool flies out and you expect some big, burly guy to be behind it, but then she jumps out and chases them. You can hardly see that thong thing she's wearing, but the sun catches it and reflects off it perfectly. After the chase, it all goes quiet and that's when I throw in my personal bit. It keeps the subscribers happy and rounds off the action."

"Hmm. There's a lot more to it then than just catching it on video. You are very clever."

"It's trial and error at first. You soon learn what works."

Gasping, Cas reached forward and pointed below the

video.

"532,667 views. What time did you upload it?"

"Two or three hours ago. If you think that's a lot, you want to see my list of subscribers. That figure there is just for starters. I don't even bother checking them anymore." Yahoo shut down the computer.

"That's incredible. You must be making a fortune from this alone."

"A small one. But that's for me to know. Do you fancy a pint?" Yahoo winked.

"I really don't want to get into the habit of going out every night."

"You'll never get your debut video sitting in your room. Not unless you get yourself a cute animal to work with and I'm afraid one of my house rules is No Pets."

Cas thought, then nodded.

"Give me twenty minutes to shower and iron a shirt and I'll come."

"I'll see you down there. For one, I don't want to miss something while waiting for you and secondly, I wouldn't want anyone getting the wrong idea."

Shrugging his shoulders, Cas walked to his room calling back, "You'd better take that apron off then."

Cas made it to The White Horse all by himself. He entered to the howling voice of a woman singing *'Band of gold'*. He glanced over to where the awful noise was coming from and spotted it was Bendy Wendy from the BEET office. Luckily she was transfixed to the karaoke screen and he made his way through the crowd to the bar without her noticing him. He found Yahoo there playing with his mobile.

"Alright! Don't tell me I missed another one," Cas said.

Yahoo flicked his phone shut and put it on the bar.

"No! Nothing's happened. I was just checking something."

He waved his finger at Lexy, but she'd already started pouring a pint for Cas. She nodded and glared between him and the pint.

He held up two fingers and she nodded and glared harder before pulling another glass from under the bar.

Cas leant in to Yahoo's ear.

"Don't say anything, but that woman singing is Bendy Wendy—my trainer at work. You know the one I told you about?"

"Yes! I know Wendy. She comes here every week, sings the same songs and gets far more flirtatious than you described." Yahoo paid for the beers.

Lexy eyed up Cas's shirt, as she gave the change and chuckled. He was flummoxed as to why, but when she turned her back, he quickly checked his buttons weren't out of line and the creases in the sleeves were hanging in the right place. Everything seemed fine, but he knew it would bug him for the rest of the evening.

He turned back to Yahoo. "I bet you get some great footage from these karaoke nights."

Yahoo gave him that 'are you dumb' look. "Do you think I'd ruin my reputation by making a karaoke video? No matter how bad or good the singers are, it's all naff and unoriginal. It's bad enough having to listen to it in a pub. No one's going to want to watch it. Don't get me wrong, there are millions of videos of 'the worst Karaoke ever'—'My dad doing this song or that'—'Karaoke duet ends in fight', blah, blah, blah. It's all crap, but if you want to video it, go ahead."

Cas didn't reply or attempt it video it. Yahoo obviously knew what he was talking about and Cas knew that if he could capture something original, Yahoo would help him and teach him to edit it to perfection. He hadn't grasped the basics yet, but he was learning all the time. He was more than eager to follow in Yahoo's footsteps, even if he didn't make a fortune, it had to be better than working in the BEET office and bluffing his way through the day. He also knew that he was bound to be caught out sooner or later and get sacked.

His thoughts were disturbed by something rubbing against his arm. It was Wendy's tit.

"Hello, my new boy."

Cas was taken aback. For a moment he thought the caramel bunny had invaded his mind. Looking round he faced the huge spider-like eyelashes of his trainer. He wondered how drunk he must be. He'd only drunk half his pint, but those lashes blinked in slow motion. Was he drugged up? He glanced back to Yahoo. His blinks were in real time. He realised it was Wendy who was off her face and her blinks were half to be seductive and half due to the fact she was struggling to keep her eyes open.

"Oh. Hello Wendy. I didn't recognise you all dressed up."

She swayed her body against him.

"Do you want me all dressed down then? Are you gonna buy me a drink for being a good teacher to you?"

"Sure I'll buy you a drink. What do you want?"

She pointed at Lexy and shouted, "She knows what I want."

Lexy gave Cas a glance of repulsion before turning to the vodka optic and serving Wendy her drink. She snatched the money from Cas's hand without even a thank you. Not wanting to upset her again, he called to her as she was about turn to the till. "Me and Yahoo too. And one for yourself."

She did a strange head wobble before continuing with

the order. Cas took his meagre change, but daren't question what she'd decided to take for her drink.

Wendy pressed closer.

"What's your name again? I *hic* forgot."

"It's Cas. Cas Howard." He felt Yahoo poke him in the side and although he flinched a little, he tried his best to ignore it.

Wendy sniggered. "Howard you fancy coming outside for a fag, Cas?"

"I don't smoke, Wendy. I told you that before."

"It didn't stop you coming out with *hic* me before."

"That was different. You were showing me the fire points and stuff."

"Don't you find it sexy in the airlock?"

"Not really. I find it quite claustrophobic to be honest."

"You like it out in the open then?"

"I told you I don't smoke."

"I wasn't talking about smoking. Guess what I saw last night?"

"I don't know. What did you see last night?"

Wendy looked around before cupping her hand and whispering into Cas's ear. "I saw the Krankies *hic* dogging."

"What?"

"The Krankies go dogging."

The DJ announced that next up was Wendy singing D.I.V.O.R.C.E. Cas pushed her away and pointed towards him.

"It's you. You're singing—get up there."

She spun around with a swaying head and stumbled towards the DJ.

Yahoo poked Cas again. "She's definitely got the hots for you, Mate. Good luck at work tomorrow."

"Very funny, Mate. I'm sure she won't remember a thing about it—if she turns in at all. I won't be mentioning it to her. I'm downing this and going home before she's finished that song. I'll catch you later or tomorrow."

Cas necked his pint and walked straight out - well before Wendy's song was over. He couldn't work out whether he felt violated or whether he was weak and not approaching the situation like a real man would. His dilemma was disturbed by a constant nagging image of what she'd said. She saw the Krankies dogging. It was a picture that he really didn't want in his head, but he kept seeing it all the way home. When he reached the door of the flat, it all made sense. This was his opportunity to get the unique video that he so needed. One that would go viral. One that would start his career to follow in Yahoo's footsteps and the video that meant he didn't have to work at the BEET office or put up with Bendy Wendy ever again. All he had to do was film it. Yahoo would help him edit it.

He lay in his bed unable to sleep. Should he run his idea past Yahoo first? It would make sense to. Yahoo might have tips for the angle or distance he'd need for a perfect shot. He decided against it afraid that he might steal the idea from him. He'd have to do research. He tried to work out a plan. First, he'd have to find out where the Krankies lived and what car they drove. Then, he'd need to know where they went dogging. There didn't seem that much to it. It was clear to him why Yahoo called these little ventures missions. This was Cas's mission and he was determined to accomplish it by himself.

When he finally slept, it wasn't at all well. His nightmares were filled with Umpa Lumpas, The Krankies and Bendy Wendy all writhing in a mass orgy in the airlock with him trapped at one end waiting for the door to click, so he could make his escape.

Mission

The following day at the BEET office he couldn't concentrate on the little work he was getting away with doing. His small hurdles of home, car and location of the previous night's plan had become huge hurdles in the light of day. He needed a plan of action rather than ideas sitting dormant in his brain. The thought had occurred to him to ask Wendy where she saw this remarkable sight, but the fear of her misinterpreting his request and seeing it as an invitation to join in, whatever she got up to, flashed through his mind. He was uneasy enough in the airlock with her. He wouldn't be able to handle sitting in her car on the way to a beauty spot for dogging sports. It wasn't only Wendy he was afraid to mention any part of his investigation to. Being new to the town, people might get suspicious of his questioning and gossip about him behind his back, branding him a weirdo of some kind. It would be hard to clear his name and what would he tell his mother if he appeared on her doorstep after being run out of the town.

His mind was racing with ideas and bad situations combined. One second he was determined to go for it, the next he was telling himself to forget the whole idea. He couldn't make his mind up either way. His frustration grew and was taken out on the callers who received groans and growls before being told to try again later.

He flicked through the internet on his mobile searching

for any information about the Krankies whereabouts while clicking through the pages on his computer screen, so at least he looked busy.

Not noticing Wendy swish past the front of his desk, hold her hands up to her face open-mouthed before shaking her head wildly at him, he continued searching.

Then it was right there in front of him. The Krankies did live in this county. It wasn't much, but it confirmed that Wendy was probably telling the truth. The thrill of the chase had him hooked, but Wendy had made her way around to him and grabbed him by the shoulder sinking her pointy red fingernails into his skin through his shirt. Cas jumped and took off his headset.

"Wendy, that hurts."

"You'll get me sacked, you will. Don't you remember what I told you about mobiles not being brought into the office?"

"No! I don't recall you mentioning my mobile at all."

She shook her head at him and bent down close to his ear. Her smooth voice was less harsh than the face she'd pulled.

"Sweetie, this is a top security office. Why do think there's an airlock, no windows and nobody using a mobile phone. What were you doing on it?"

"I was checking my mail. I didn't get the chance to this morning."

"So, you haven't taken any pictures in here? None of the computer screens?"

"No! Why would I want to do that?"

"There is extremely sensitive information that criminals would find most useful to them on these computers."

"Come on, Wendy. I wouldn't even know where to find it even if I wanted to."

"Well, it has to go. Either don't bring it into work at all

or leave it with the security guard at reception in the morning. He'll put it in a locker for you. Do not ever bring it in here again. You're lucky it's me that spotted it and not the manager else we'd both be sacked by now. Take it to reception and don't let me see it in here again, you hear?"

"I'm sorry." Cas got up and headed for the door.

"Cas!" Wendy hollered at him, though not a soul in the office flinched from their stations or even looked up.

Cas spun around to see her with one hand on her hip and the other pointing at his computer. He rushed back to her.

"I'm sorry. Yes, I remember you telling me to switch it off if I leave it. It just slipped my mind in the rush."

As he locked his computer, she leant her bosom on his shoulder and whispered in his ear, "And make it quick or your stats will suffer. I'll be watching you more closely from now on."

That confirmed it for him. There was no way ever that he'd be asking her about her experience with the Krankies.

The rest of the day was frustrating and dragged so slowly. Cas had a lead. He was one step closer to mission accomplished. He worked out what step two would be without having to involve Wendy. What he needed was a postman. If he could find the Krankies address, he could easily find what car they drove. He needed some local information on where people went dogging and he was sure he could get that out of some of the guys at The White Horse if he approached the subject as a joke. What kind of joke he didn't know, but that was way down his list of priorities for now along with one other. How would he get there was his last dilemma of the plan. He couldn't drive, but he remembered Yahoo's offer of his scooter. It would be a little odd arriving at a dogging scene on a scooter, but it was his only option. Once there, the rest would be simple. These dogging people would be happily doing what they do, on show for everyone to see or film.

His mind had got way ahead of him again. He was no nearer to actually achieving any of the steps, but the fact that he'd conceived the notion and contrived a feasible plan, all by himself, gave him an electric thrill of success.

He worked through the rest of the day suppressing his frustration by imagining his plan as a list and ticking off each box, as he got closer to mission accomplished. Envisaging that that would be how it would happen in reality, once he could get out of this office, he rose above his pessimism and dispelled his negative fears, until he was through the airlock. Now that he had the time to work through his list for real, it didn't seem so easy.

Collecting his mobile from the security guard, he called his mother. He didn't tell her of his mission, only that things were going well and would, hopefully, soon get even better.

Hanging up and walking home his heart sank. He would never be able to tell his mother about his success. He could turn up in a flash car with presents for her, but it didn't seem right to tell her how he'd come about his wealth. She was quite a fan of the Krankies and she'd be sure to want to see the video. He doubted she even knew what dogging was. He shrugged off the thought of her disapproval and disappointment in him. He could tell her he'd risen through the ranks and was one of the top men at the BEET office. If he stayed in Berrycroft with Yahoo, she would never be any the wiser.

Realising he was daydreaming about the wrong end of his plan, he went back to the beginning. A postman was what he needed. He'd ask Yahoo what time the postman came, as it was a perfectly innocent question, and he'd try to catch him on Saturday. It seemed so far away and how would he approach the subject? He wasn't sure that the postman was even allowed to divulge such information as people's addresses. He figured he might have to bribe him.

Walking into the flat with a head that was about to explode, he was hit by a familiar smell.

"Smells great," he said, stepping into the kitchen.

"Tomato and tuna pasta bake with a garlic and mozzarella topping. You look exhausted. What have they been doing to you down that place?"

"Oh, nothing any different from any other day. I got a telling off, so I'm pretty pissed off. You know I can't take my phone into the office. Not that anything would likely happen there anyway, but it would be just my luck that it did and I'd be unable to film it."

"No way! A full day without your phone. That would kill me. You're gonna have to find another job."

"I'm working on it, believe me. I think I've figured my role in that place. It's to produce stats. No one seems to care about what work I'm supposed to be doing, but they are very concerned about stats. Sadly, I don't share their enthusiasm of them, as much as they'd like me to. I'd much rather do some proper work."

"That's great. That means you're a stat-producing chicken. That's better than yesterday when you were an unproductive chicken. You are going up in the world, my friend. Here, tuck in."

A plate was slid in front of him and a basket of garlic bread was placed on the table.

Enjoying his meal, but getting a little sick of pasta, Cas changed the subject, as Yahoo didn't take his gripes seriously anyway.

"Where did you learn to cook so well? You said you had no qualifications, and I know you don't need them to cook, but your meals are delicious and always cooked to perfection."

"It's quite a long and sad story really, but I'll tell you anyway. I had a crush on this Italian girl when I was at school. She was the most beautiful creature I'd ever seen and her voice, well her accent, just melted my whole body when she spoke. Being shy, I found it difficult to look at her, let alone speak to her, but I was determined to get over it somehow. I had an image of her eating out in fancy restaurants every night, so I got myself a part time job in an Italian bistro in the hope that she'd come in one night and I could impress her. I was merely a skivvy at first, but I watched how they made stuff and asked a lot of questions. Soon they were letting me help the chef and as time went on, I got pretty good. She never did come into the bistro, so I changed my plan. Having more confidence in myself, thanks to being around the waitresses, I decided I was going to ask her to dinner one night at my mum's house and make sure she saw I'd cooked everything myself. I wanted it to be perfect, so I waited and learnt more until I was almost as good as the chef. I guess I waited too long and spent so many hours in the bistro that I missed the boat. When I finally had the courage to ask her, she was gone. One of her friends told me that she'd moved back to Italy and married some Mafia guy. I thought it best not to pursue her. I realised then that life is too short to plan too far ahead. If you wanna do something, just do it or the opportunity could be gone."

A chord struck in Cas's brain and although the tale was sad and romantic, it was lost on him. Saturday was too long to wait for the postman. He tried his best to stay in the flow of the conversation.

"Hmm. You have a good point there. You never wanted to be a chef then?"

"Oh, and I thought my story might make you shed a

tear. You're a hard man, Cas. And hell no, did I want to be a chef! They work ridiculous hours trapped in a scorching kitchen. I like being free too much. I cook purely for pleasure for my friends. You do enjoy my cooking, don't you?"

His craving for a plate of beans and chips made Cas pause for thought. He stuffed a forkful of pasta into his mouth and made a yum-yum noise nodding his head.

Yahoo held up his thumb.

"That's good. I get quite sick of pasta myself, but I don't know how to cook anything else."

Cas spluttered on his food and Yahoo jumped up to thump him on the back. Waving his arm, Cas gestured that he was okay and swallowed the obstruction away.

"It went down the wrong hole, Mate. No worries. Do you know any postmen round here?"

"What's that got to do with you choking on my cooking?"

"Nothing at all. It just came to mind. I thought it would be a better job than being trapped in that office without my mobile. You know, I'd be out on the streets all day and might catch some worthy footage."

"Good thinking, Cas. You're getting the idea. There is Bob in the pub—he's a postman. He's a bit odd though. You might have seen him. He sits in the corner with a book and rarely talks to anyone. He's in there most afternoons and goes home early. I guess he has to if he has to get up at ridiculous o'clock."

Cas couldn't believe his luck. A major step of his plan was within reach and sitting there waiting for him in The White Horse. Yahoo's magic did seem to be rubbing off on him after all. He scoffed what was left of his meal.

"I'll get changed and pop down there now then. Are you coming down? Silly question I know."

"I will be later. I'm gonna take a drive down to the skate park. I have a feeling." Yahoo gave a cheeky smile and a wink before licking his plate clean.

Cas wondered whether the Italian girl would have been as impressed with Yahoo's table manners as she would have been with his culinary skills. He couldn't bring himself to lick his own plate, but Yahoo did it as if it was all part of the process of dining. Maybe it was in Italy. Not having ever been to an Italian restaurant, Cas couldn't know.

"I'll catch you later then."

Showered and changed in record speed, Cas continued on his mission to introduce himself to Bob. He hadn't figured out how he was going to get the information out of the guy, but the way his luck was going, Bob might just tell him outright.

Striding towards the pub, Cas focused on the doorway and muttered to himself, "Don't leave before I get there."

Entering as normally as he could, he scanned the room and walked towards his now usual spot at the bar. There was only one guy reading a book and he was kind of in the corner. He had a full pint of Guinness on his table.

Lexy had already started pulling a pint.

Cas raised his arm. "I was going to try a Guinness."

"If you want good service, don't be swapping your drinks around. You can have a Guinness next round alright." She puckered her lips tight showing she'd already won the argument.

He didn't dare complain. Leaning against the bar, so he had Bob within eyeshot, he paid for his lager and deliberated about how he was going to introduce himself.

The guy sipped at his Guinness extremely slowly, but flicked through the pages of his book at a tremendous rate. He looked rather odd. He had a small frame and a very large forehead with one thick eyebrow stretching straight across it. At first glance, Cas had thought it was the rim of his glasses, but as Bob tipped his head back to swig and then dropped his face into his book, it was clear it wasn't attached to his spectacles.

Biding his time, Cas made small talk with Lexy hoping to fish for some information.

"What you got on tonight then?"

"Well, this is a nylon blouse that I got down the market. The black skirt is ..."

"Very funny. I meant what have you got on in the pub? There always seems to be something going on here."

"I know what you meant. Men's darts league. Do you want to join? They are always a man short, so they never win."

"I think I'll give it a miss. I inherited my mother's genes when it comes to aiming and throwing. They'd probably kick me out for being a girl."

Scowling at him Lexy replied, "The ladies' darts is in tomorrow night, but I doubt they'd appreciate your skill or your comment. They haven't lost a game this season."

Wondering how this girl could make him feel so uncomfortable, whatever he said, Cas changed the subject. He noticed the jukebox was next to where Bob was seated.

"It's pretty quiet in here. I'll stick some tunes on. Any requests?"

Lexy shook her head.

"Not from me, but if you want to upset Bob, put anything on except Simon and Garfunkel, or Leonard Cohen."

He frowned for a moment while he grasped what she really meant, before going over to the jukebox and receiving a filthy, flighty look from Bob.

Cas chose well. As the first few bars of the song pumped out, the beady eyes of Bob turned straight to him. A cheesy grin spread across his face and even his eyebrow gave a smile. Nodding his recognition of a fellow soul with great taste, Cas returned to the bar proud that his forethought had made his coming introduction much easier for him.

"Lexy, can I have that Guinness now?" He downed the lager and waited for his second reason to have an affinity with Bob to be placed in front of him. He waited a long while, but the timing couldn't have been better. Lexy placed the pint in front of Cas a moment before Bob got out of his chair and walked towards the bar with his empty glass. Cas took his chance.

"I'll get this man's too. It's good to meet someone who appreciates good music."

Bob shook his head. A gentle, timid voice replied, "No. Please don't. I'm going after this one. I don't want to get into a round."

"Don't be daft, Man. You don't have to get me one back. I'm Cas. What are you reading?"

"Okay, Cas. I'm Bob. It would be rude of me not to accept, but I'll buy you one next time I see you. The book—it's *The Dice Man*. Have you read it?"

Thanking his stars that Bob hadn't got into a conversation about Leonard Cohen, who Cas knew nothing about, he paid for the beer. Never having read the book, he decided not to lie that he had.

"I can't say I have. Is it any good?"

"It's fabulous. It's truly enlightening. I've almost finished it. When I have, I'll leave it behind the bar for you if you like—you're very welcome to borrow it."

"Cheers, Mate. What do you get up to then—when you're not in here?"

"Not much except work. I'm a postman ..."

"Really!"

Cas listened looking intensely interested in Bob's run-through of his day from the time his alarm went off in the morning and through all his gripes of how things had changed and him having to do overtime to keep himself in an enjoyable pint or two after work. There wasn't even a biting dog story in the man.

Yahoo bounced in through the door and exclaimed, "Yahoo. Pint, Lexy and whatever he's drinking. Hi Bob! Are you staying for another?"

Bob shrank away muttering, "No thanks, must go now." He tucked his book under his arm and left.

Cas was slightly disappointed that he hadn't got to ask him the question, but he sensed the man was very private and he wasn't going to divulge people's addresses that easily. He knew he'd made a good first impression on Bob and with a little more work he would get it out of the man and reach his goal.

With Bob out of the building, Lexy served Yahoo and tilted her head at Cas.

"What will it be this time? A white wine spritzer? A Babycham maybe?"

"Same as him thanks," Cas said, nodding towards Yahoo.

She got on with pouring it while Yahoo questioned Cas.

"Well, can he get you a job at the post office?"

"We didn't get that far. I think you scared him off."

"I told you he was odd."

"I'm working on it. He's lending me a book."

"Oh! You work fast. He must like you—he treasures those books, you know? I thought you wanted a job though. How did you end up with a book instead?"

"I didn't want the guy to think I was harassing him—he

seems quite delicate, so I thought I'd just be friendly for starters."

"And what did I tell you about missing the boat?"

"I could have got further if you hadn't come tearing in and frightening the poor man."

"Okay, blame me. What's the book about?"

"I don't know—I didn't get that far. He said it was brilliant. It's called *The Dice Man*."

Yahoo gasped and held up his hands as if he was backing away from a wild beast.

"Be very, very careful with that. It's a proper head-fuck of a book. It's one of those that'll make you or break you."

Lexy gave Cas his pint and nodded in agreement.

"Or it'll send you totally do-lally. He caught me a treat when he came in today."

Yahoo paid. "Tell us more."

"He asked me how I was, as he usually does. I told him I was fine, but didn't know what to do for the darts team's food tonight. I'm always giving them sausages and chips and to be honest, they don't seem to mind, but I end up stinking of fat all night. It gets into my clothes and my hair and it's just plain revolting. Anyhow, he got out this dice, a pen and paper, and asked me what two things would be acceptable to the dart players and me. I told him—a tray of mixed sandwiches or a shepherd's pie. He wrote them down with the numbers 3 and 4 written next to them. Then, he asked me what would be acceptable for them, but ridiculous for me to do. I said spending a hundred pounds on a mixed pizza delivery and creating a Christmas dinner with all the trimmings. He wrote those as 1 and 2. Then he asked, what would be easy for me but unacceptable for them. I thought about it for a while and said bananas and custard or muesli which became 5 and 6. Anyway, then he says that I never realised just how many options I had got until then and to leave it for the dice to decide. He rolls the dice and it's a 5—bananas and custard—he claimed my problem is solved. Like I'm going to give the darts players bananas and custard. They'll think I've gone bananas."

Cas was trying to get his head around all she was saying, but Yahoo pointed out what even she was missing.

"If you don't give them bananas and custard you will feel like a failure. You played the game. The decision was taken out of your hands and down to the roll of the die. And it's die for one die, dice for two. The thing is unless you give them what the die said, you'll never experience the point that this book is making."

"But I can't give them bananas and custard."

"Why can't you? What's stopping you?"

"Well, nothing is stopping me except my own sense."

"Do them sausage and chips then and stop complaining, but you'll never understand the concept if you do."

"I don't want to do bloody sausage and chips."

"Do what the die told you then, otherwise, it'll bug you forever. They won't die from eating bananas and custard. It's quite a tame choice considering you could have said arsenic-laced soup."

Lexy walked away looking perplexed.

Cas still couldn't see the point.

"So, if she had said arsenic-laced soup and the die had fell on that, would you still be telling her to do it?"

"Theoretically, yes. You have to have read the book to understand and I would seriously advise you against it."

Not liking the sound of it, Cas didn't pry any further, but changed the subject.

"You came in full of yourself. Did some kid fall off his skateboard?"

"Oh, Cas. Do you really think I'd waste my time with such trivial fails? I thought that's all I was getting at first, but then it went quite bizarre. I'll show you tomorrow when I've edited it."

"No! Please tell me now. I've spent the last hour listening about Bob's day and getting black looks from Lexy. I could do with a laugh."

"It'll be funnier if you watch it."

"I don't care. I'll still watch it tomorrow. Just tell me what happened?"

"Okay! I got down to the skate park and the usual skaters were doing their stuff. Then some kids I'd never seen before turned up and they'd nicked one of those swan boats from the lake and brought it with them. Somehow, they managed to get it up on top of one of the ramps, with the help of the others, and then jumped in it. They rocked it on the edge until it slipped off. I could see it wasn't going to end happily and I thought it'd only be any good for a compilation. Anyway, what you'd expect to happen happened. They went careering down the ramp at quite a speed and up the other side where the thing flipped over and they went flying out in all directions. Funnyish! Then it got bizarre. There is a lone, real swan that lives on that lake. I'd heard a story about, it a while back, that it had fallen in love with one of the swan boats and stayed by its side when people took it out for a ride. That must have been the boat that the kids nicked because this swan came out of nowhere, hissing and flapping its wings at the kids. They all started screaming and running in all directions. It was really attacking the poor little buggers and I did get quite concerned at one point. I've heard those things can break a man's arm. I told you it wasn't that funny. You'll have to wait until I've edited it, but the moment will be spoiled."

"No! It is funny. I'm just flabbergasted that you're always there at the right time."

Yahoo slapped Cas on the knee. "I told you, Mate. I can sense these things."

"So what happened? Were all the kids okay?"

"They were fine—just a bit shook up. It wasn't that heavy at all just a fibreglass shell, so I dragged the swan boat back to the lake with that hissing swan following me, but he calmed down once she was back in the water. Anyhow, job done for today—let's drink."

"I'm not having anymore. My stomach feels a bit odd and I've got work in the morning. I've already had one more than I promised myself."

Yahoo tutted. "You shouldn't mix Guinness with lager. You'll learn. I'll see you later, maybe."

Nodding and pushing away the remainder of his pint Cas replied, "Good night, Mate. I'll see you tomorrow. I'm having an early night."

"Okay. Roll on the weekend."

"Talking of the weekend, would it be alright if I dragged your scooter out and checked it over? I might need it if I get a job at the post office."

"So long as you don't sell it, you're welcome to do what you like with it. Can you smell custard?"

Cas sniffed the air. "Yes or maybe I'm imagining it with all that talk. Goodnight."

Once home Cas spent the rest of the evening in bed watching Yahoo's videos and trying to figure out what made them stand heads above all the millions of other videos available. He knew Yahoo was choosy about what he posted and his sense of timing was perfect for the ultimate laugh, but there was something more. There was something very Yahoo about all his videos. Cas knew that if he watched a bunch at random, without knowing who'd made them, he'd be able to pick out those that Yahoo had created. He'd nailed it. The guy had style and a unique one at that. This worried Cas. He had an ingenious plan, but he doubted he had any style.

His nightmares took him to a store where he hunted for style while Umpa Lumpas ran around laughing hysterically at him.

Contact

More than half a week into his new job and Cas was still managing to blag his way through the day with no questions asked.

Boredom was making the hours drag though, so today he made a real effort to get his head around what the point of his job was, apart from stats, and to see if he could do some actual productive work. The idea being that if he was busy the time might go faster. He didn't get very far, but it broke the tedium and time sped up slightly for a while. His mind was soon back to The Krankies. He tried his best not to get carried away to the place at the end of his mission and keep it in real time. He had to get over the first hurdle - the address. If he concentrated on that and that alone, he would get at least one box ticked. It was all about Bob. Somehow he had to get the guy to trust him. He knew how skittish he was and that if he went in for the kill, he could ruin his chances of getting the required info. He also knew that the BEET office was taking up valuable time and if he didn't get the address before the weekend that step two would be put back maybe another week. He had to be gentle, but he needed that address before Saturday. He started to slip ahead of himself. He'd get the scooter started on Saturday and he'd go to the address and see what car they drove. Then - then he realised he was doing it again. He rewound his brain back to Bob and started at the beginning and so the cycle continued until it was time to leave the BEET office.

Desperate to get to the pub and meet Bob, he jogged home from work. He could smell something Italian, as he opened the flat door, and it didn't smell so good anymore. To his surprise Yahoo had made pizza. It was a welcome change from pasta, but apart from the lack of pasta, it was all the same ingredients thrown on top of a flatbread.

"Good day?" Yahoo asked.

"Same as always. Did nothing—bored out of my brains and my eyes and ears sting from staring at that pointless screen and hearing all those desperate voices that mean nothing to me. I've gotta get out of there. I'm going straight to the pub after this. I need to spend some time with Bob."

"Why don't you just apply to the post office and leave Bob out of it?"

"Erm ... Do you know how many jobs I've applied for and failed even to get an interview? Hmm, nor do I. It's hundreds if not thousands. My mother told me to do it the old way. Meet someone that'll help you get in some place. That's what I'm doing and it's good advice. It got me a place to stay."

"Don't you want to see my swan video before you go? I know it didn't sound like much, but I've edited it around the Swan Lake ballet music. It's so weird now. It's funny, violent, and I kept the part in when I took her back to the water, so I'm the hero and it has a happy ending. I'm not sure what the original story for Swan Lake was, but it's really something special now."

Cas threw down his last crust and wondered if Yahoo would finish off by licking his plate, even though there'd only be a few crumbs and some crusts. He didn't have the patience to wait and see.

"Maybe I'll watch it later. Bob doesn't hang around for long. I want to get right in with him. Please don't be bursting in and scaring him off too soon."

Without even changing out of his office clothes, Cas was out of the door in a shot.

Entering The White Horse in a casual manner, Cas nodded an acknowledgment to Bob as he walked up to the bar. Immediately, Bob came rushing over to his side.

"I'll get this one. I owe you one."

"Hey, calm down Bob. You don't have to. It doesn't work like that."

"I want to. I'm sorry," Bob said.

"You have nothing to apologise for either. Look if you want to buy me a drink, that's fine by me. Thank you very much."

"I'm sorry. You're very welcome."

Bob placed the right change on the bar and shuffled back to his corner.

Lexy gave Cas an unwelcoming smile.

"I saw your head bobbing along past the window, but I didn't start pouring your drink. What would you be drinking today, I wonder?"

As much as Cas wanted a Guinness to impress his new comrade, he thought better of it.

"I'll stick to the lager from now on, thanks. How did the darts go?"

"They lost as usual. Man short, as usual."

"I meant the food. What did you do for them in the end?"

She started chuckling.

"I did it. I gave them bananas and custard. I was really worried about what they'd say, but I didn't feel at all responsible. It wasn't my choice after all—it was the dice's choice. I was all ready to blame the dice, but amazingly they loved it. It reminded them of being at school and they had a big debate afterwards about all the nice stuff they used to eat when they were young that they wouldn't dream of making or ordering now. It made me feel great and that reminds me—Bob gave me the book to put behind the bar in case he missed you, but I asked him if I could read it first. He said we had to sort it out between ourselves, as he doesn't like getting involved in conflicts. Now, what is it they say about the law? Possession is such and such, and I'm in possession of it, so you'll have to wait."

Sniffing and turning his nose up, Cas turned towards the jukebox, harping back at Lexy. "I'm quite capable of going into a book shop and buying a copy if I wanted it that much."

He tried to choose some different Leonard Cohen from the day before, but as he had never heard any of them and Bob seemed grateful for anything he chose, he tapped in the numbers picking every other song on the play-list.

Then sitting down at Bob's table, he asked if he minded.

Bob shook his head. "A Leonard Cohen fan is always welcome at my table."

Changing the subject for fear of being exposed, Cas turned it to books.

"I said Lexy could read that book first. She seems quite spellbound by that dice thing."

Bob nodded with a thoughtful look that spread into an uncharacteristic, devilish smile.

"I've spent my life keeping myself to myself and worrying about how people perceive me, what kind of reputation I have and what repercussions my actions might cause me or others. I have to say that book is fantastic. I finished it only an hour ago and I feel quite liberated. It's a strange experience."

"That good, ay? Well you know what Bob, although I haven't read the book yet, I did get the rundown of the dice thing from Lexy and Yahoo. I thought I'd give it a go, as it's my mum's birthday next weekend, and so I wrote a list—one to six of presents I could get her. I chose some she'd hate, the usual stuff and a couple of things that seemed impossible, but that I know she'd love. That is how it works, right?"

Bob's eyes grew wide. "You've got the gist of it. Did you leave it up to the dice to decide?"

"I did, Bob. And do you know what it told me to get her?"

"No! Tell me."

"It told me to get her The Krankies autographs. Now what am I supposed to do? I've got a week and it's surely impossible."

Clapping his hands and shaking his head, Bob sat tall in his chair.

"Nothing is impossible. That's the magic. If it's been chosen for you, you have to find a way to do it. I just so happen to know where The Krankies live. I used to deliver their mail, but they moved. Of course, I know their forwarding address."

Cas pulled the best amazed face he could muster.

"You're kidding me, surely? This is unreal. My mum is a massive fan of The Krankies and it would make her year if I got her an autograph. I would never have dreamt of attempting such a present. Thank you, Bob. Can I have the address?"

"I don't know it off the top of my head. I'll find it at work tomorrow. In fact, why don't you come to mine for dinner tomorrow night? I might have something even better than that for you."

Cas couldn't find a reason to refuse. He had to go along with Bob until he had that address in his hand. He wondered what could be even better than The Krankies autograph, but he could think of millions of things.

"I'd love to, Bob. That's really kind of you." As Cas imagined Bob being a fish and chip kind of guy on a Friday, he started to look forward to it.

Bob took a die from his pocket and a list numbered one to six.

"Just testing to see what I should read next. Tossing the die across the table, they both peered at the result. It was a five. Bob held his head in his hands. "No!"

Scanning the list and wondering what book could be so bad, Cas read out loud. "Get a Kindle."

"That and the Bible were my bad ones. The one thing I've always said I would never do is get a Kindle. Books are meant to be real, stroked, touched and smelt. I must do it though—it will only depress me if I fail to follow my fate. I only need to read one book on it. Then I'll go back to real books. It's a challenge alright and a nasty one at that, but I have to do it. I will do it."

Cas couldn't see what the big deal was, but it was obviously very disconcerting for Bob.

"I think you're taking it a little too seriously. Why not toss it again? We'll say that one was a miss-throw."

"Dear Cas, it doesn't work like that. I couldn't live with myself if I did that. I wrote the choices and the die decided. I'll do it, and who knows? There may be a reason why I threw a five. I'm going to leave you now. I'm sorry I can't stay longer, but I've much to do and I have to go and order that Kindle before it preys on mind too long."

"Sure, I understand."

Bob scribbled his address on the back of the book list. "I'll see you tomorrow. Is six o'clock okay?"

"That suits me fine. I'll bring some beer."

"No! No. It's my treat. Don't you worry about bringing anything. I'll have it all in hand. See you tomorrow, my friend."

"Yeah. Bye, Bob."

As Bob left, Cas went back to his spot at the bar.

"What is it you're up to?" Lexy asked.

"And what is that supposed to mean?"

"Dunno really. Aren't you happy at Yahoo's? Are you looking to move in with Bob? He's a very lonely man and I bet he's looking for company. I'd say he'd be very choosy on his choice of lodger. It would have to be someone that understands him, has the same tastes in music and likes talking about books. Think of the lovely evenings and weekends you'd have together. I heard he was married years ago, but I'm not sure what happened. It's just him rattling around in a big, cold house now. I bet he'd look after you really well."

Cas looked a little worried. "Stop it, will you? I'm more than happy at Yahoo's flat. I have been invited round to Bob's tomorrow night for dinner, that's all. You don't really think he wants me to move in, do you?"

Lexy sniggered and started to pour a pint.

Yahoo slapped Cas on the back.

"Who's trying to poach my lodger?"

"Jesus! Yahoo. Where did you come from?"

"I crept in as quietly as I could. I didn't want to frighten your new little friend."

"Don't you start. He's gone anyway."

"Did you mention the post office job?"

"No, not yet."

"So what was that I caught about him wanting you to move in with him?"

Shaking his head, Cas pointed at Lexy.

"He doesn't. She's winding me up again, Man. Bob's invited me for dinner tomorrow night. That is all."

"Nice one. That was quick going of you. You'll be in that post office in no time."

Lexy raised her eyebrows and threw a wise nod Cas's way, as she handed them both a pint.

A bedraggled-looking man in a stretched holey jumper appeared behind the bar, bent down, grabbed a handful of stuff, including a bottle of whisky, and disappeared without a word back to where he'd come from.

Cas stared at Lexy. "Don't tell me that is your boyfriend?"

"Is it heck. That's the damn Landlord. The guy that's supposed to be running this place."

"I've never seen him before. I did wonder if there was someone higher in charge or if it was all down to you, but I didn't want to pry."

"It is all down to me. The lazy bastard sits upstairs drinking all day and night. Every day, since I started, he's put more and more jobs on me. The cleaner walked out on him and instead of getting another one, he told me to come in a couple of hours earlier and do it. That was handy for him cos it means I'm here to take the deliveries, open the back gate for the rubbish men, let in the machine guys, stock-taker and whoever fancies a drink before opening time. He does absolutely nothing. I do it all and yet my money hasn't gone up once. The only good thing about it is—he keeps out of my way and I'm glad he rarely comes behind the bar because he stinks ..."

Yahoo butted in. "This pub was shit before you started though, Lexy. Hardly anyone ever came in and those that did weren't welcomed by the man. I got the impression that he didn't want any customers at all. It's great now and the best place for him is upstairs or does he squat down in the cellar? That's where he looks like he lives."

"Bastard!" Lexy exclaimed.

Yahoo looked shocked. "I was only saying that ..."

"No! Not you. Him! The bastard has not only took a litre and a half bottle of whisky, but he's taken my book."

Cas coughed. "My book."

Yahoo nudged him. "Would that be Bob's book?"

"Okay, Bob's book."

Shaking his head, Yahoo tutted. "Dear, oh dear. I told you that book can be dangerous in the wrong hands and you're both squabbling over it. One of you will regret reading it. Mark my word."

There was a screeching of brakes from outside. Yahoo spun around holding up his phone. Cas knew he should do the same, but it felt silly to and he was mesmerised by the sight of a lorry heading straight for the pub. In a split second the truck hit the building, the driver flew through the windscreen, the pub window, somersaulted in the air and miraculously landed on his feet in front of them.

All were silent before Cas stuttered, "Sh,sh,shit."

Lexy held up her hands. "I guess I better call the glaziers. Does it never end?"

Yahoo kept filming.

The driver turned around and looked at the scene he'd created. Feeling his face and head, and looking at his hands for signs of blood, he began to laugh.

Cas got a chair and placed it behind him.

"Sit down, Man. You look fine. There's not a scratch on you, but you never know what kind of damage you might have done internally."

He called over to Lexy who was on the phone.

"I think you should call an ambulance before the glaziers."

She threw him a filthy look. "I am. You are such a dick

sometimes."

Switching off his mobile, Yahoo patted the guy on the shoulder. "You are one lucky man. If you'd hit the wall instead of the window, your skull would be in bits now. That was some acrobatic feat."

The driver frowned at him.

"What's that supposed to mean? One second I'm swerving from hitting this guy in the road—the next I'm standing here in front of you lot."

"I'll show you. Let me just slow it down."

Yahoo handed him his mobile and the driver's face lit up as he watched.

"Wow! That is brilliant. I couldn't have done that if I'd tried. Show me it again."

They ran through the video quite a few times before the driver had seen it enough. He was laughing with relief and didn't seem to have inflicted any injury at all, not even shock.

"I hope you'll put that on the internet. I've gotta get all my mates to see this."

Smiling a 'pleased with himself' grin, Yahoo nodded.

"It would be my pleasure. I'll do it tonight. I'll call it *Most impressive way to enter a pub ever.* It won't be hard to find."

"Thank you. It's a shame you didn't get what happened a few seconds earlier. It would save me trying to explain it to the police."

Cas noticed blue lights flashing outside. "It looks like they're here. What did happen?"

"A really small guy dressed as Batman walked straight out in front of me. I don't think he did it on purpose. I'd say he couldn't see where he was going in that silly mask. As I swerved to miss him and mounted the pavement, there was a cat sitting there watching him. I should just have ran it over and I wouldn't have hit the pub. Stupidly I veered away from it and lost control."

"Well, luckily you're okay and so is the cat and so is Batman. I think you should go to the hospital and get checked over, though." Cas said, as an paramedic and a police officer entered the pub.

The driver was escorted straight to the ambulance and Yahoo and Cas went back to supping their beer while Lexy rang the glaziers.

"You were quick on the draw with that one," Cas said.

"It becomes automatic. My mobile often beats my eyes to things," Yahoo replied.

"Do you think that guy is really alright? All that stuff about Batman makes me think he might have some brain damage."

"Look. Watch the video in really slow-motion. The pub window and his windscreen both shattered on impact. He didn't hit his head on anything. He flew though a shower of fragments, so I can't see how he'd get brain-damaged."

As Cas scrutinised the video, he saw that Yahoo was right.

"He's as lucky as you."

"I've never hit a pub with a lorry and been catapulted across a room and if I had, I wouldn't consider myself at all lucky."

"I didn't mean it like that. Look, he's got away unscathed and you've got yourself another classic video from just lifting your arm. That's what I meant."

"Hmm. I wish I'd got the Batman guy as well. Even I don't have the power to be in two places at once, though. I'm happy I got the best end of the event."

Lexy held out a sweeping brush and a dust pan to Cas.

"Do me a favour and sweep that glass up. I can't do everything and there's a nosy crowd building up. I'm going to be busy this evening."

"Sure, I will. I can't believe the Landlord hasn't even come down after that racket."

"I'd say he's out cold after drinking that bottle of whisky. If they move that lorry and the glaziers fix the window tonight, he'll never know a thing about it."

The glass cleaned up, Cas said his goodbyes.

When he got back to his room, he stood in front of the mirror with his mobile in his pocket and practised his quick draw techniques before going to bed.

Bob

The nightshift workers were leaving the BEET office as Cas arrived. They looked more zombie-like than usual, but Cas guessed working nights would take its toll on any man by the end of the week. He hadn't bothered bringing his mobile in, as it seemed pointless to queue up to leave it with the security guard. Tempting fate he could be, but he hadn't missed anything significant on the way to work and he doubted he would on the way home either. His mission was his key to success and silly incidents didn't seem that important in the scheme of things. They always eluded him anyway.

Wendy was waiting for the airlock door to click.

"Morning, Wendy."

"Good morning, Cas. Just the person I need to see. I keep meaning to catch you—then it goes totally out of my head."

"Is something wrong?"

"Well, yes. It's not your fault, though. You haven't been putting your hand in the scanner when you arrive and when you leave."

"What scanner?"

"Didn't I tell you about the hand scanner? Didn't anyone?"

"No. That's the first I've heard about it."

The door clicked and they walked in.

"Well, you need to use it or you won't get paid. Payroll

won't have any record of you being here this week."

"Surely, you can tell them that I have and what hours I've done?"

"I will do my best to get it sorted out, but it's all computerised and you must know how hard it is to override a system that is made not to be corrupted."

The second door opened and Wendy walked into the office and pointed to a small box on the wall.

"Put your hand in. Type in your employee number and that's it." She demonstrated.

Cas did as he was told.

"So will you be able to sort it out before payday?"

"I doubt it very much, but if you're lucky, it'll be on next months. It'll be like having a little bonus by then."

Trying hard to smile, Cas went to his work station and started everything up. He wasn't miffed that he'd worked all week and probably wouldn't see the money for two, maybe three months if he was lucky; he was disappointed that every day his job became shittier in one way or another.

The computer fired up and told him he had mail. He clicked on it and was relieved it was 'to all' and not him personally.

'I'm sad to inform you all that Ken, the first-aider from team two, went into a coma and died whilst on night shift last night. This means team two is without a first-aider which is required by law. If anyone has a first aid certificate or would like to spend an hour this afternoon to gain one and join team two - please reply ASAP.'

Cas read it through twice. He was well aware that he had a first-aider certificate, but he had to weigh up the pros and cons before rushing in. In one respect it would make him look good in the company's eyes. He'd be bailing them out of a problem and it could go in his favour for any future promotions. On the other hand, he'd seen the state of the night shift workers. They were even paler than the day shift and looked like they could sleep all day. The dilemma of what was most important in his life played on his mind for about four seconds. The Krankies or work.

He deleted the email. Team two could die one by one without his aid, as far as he was concerned.

The rest of the day could only be described as painful. Apart from it dragging, the sound of the office resembled a chicken shed. He wasn't sure if something had changed. Maybe it was that there were more women working in this team or maybe it was Yahoo's jibe and he was actually going slightly mad.

Moments before the end of his shift another email popped up asking if anyone wanted to work the weekend. He deleted it and shut down his computer.

Remembering, as he left the building, that he was meant to swipe his hand before exiting the office, he continued on his way home. There was no way he was going back into that place and he figured the computer might calculate his wages for the whole weekend, as it would have no record of him leaving.

Back at the flat, Cas showered and ironed his clothes. There was no tomato and garlic smell, but a whiff of charcoal in the air.

Standing in the hallway, he tweaked at his fringe while posing in front of the mirror. Yahoo appeared from his office and laughed at him.

"You're definitely dressed to impress. I hope Bob doesn't get the wrong idea."

"Don't be daft. He seems an alright guy really. He just looks a bit odd. That's not his fault. Is something on fire?"

"I don't think so. I had some toast earlier. I couldn't see the point of doing dinner, as you've got a date."

"Stop it."

"I thought I'd have a session tonight if you want to meet me in The Horse later and tell me how you got on."

"Sure. I'll only be a couple of hours. I guess he goes to bed early."

"He might already be there waiting for you."

"Will you stop? I'll see you later."

"Good luck," called Yahoo, as Cas walked out the door.

Bob's house wasn't that far from the flat, but it was no comparison. It was a big, old town house. The window frames hadn't seen paint for years and the varnish was peeling on the front door. Cas rapped the old knocker.

The door opened almost immediately and Bob stood and stared for a second before taking a small bow.

"Welcome to my humble abode, Cas. Please come in."

Following behind Bob through the hallway and into the sitting room, Cas was amazed by the amount of books Bob had collected. Every wall was floor to ceiling with bookshelves stuffed with books in no particular order, size or age.

"Wow, Bob. Have you read all these?"

"All at least once. Please sit down and I'll fetch you a glass of wine. Red or white?"

Not knowing much about wine and not really liking it, Cas went for the easy option. "Whatever you recommend, Bob. I know you have good taste."

"Red it is then." Bob left the room and a cat entered. It made a noise unlike any cat Cas had met before. A deep wail, more like a moo than a mew, left its scabby mouth.

Under his breath, Cas whispered, "Hello, Puss. Don't come any closer."

Bob reappeared with two glasses of wine and sat on the armchair opposite Cas. The cat jumped up into his lap and mooed again. Bob stroked it from the tip of its nose to the end of its tail, as its body stretched and writhed. The action had no smoothing effect on the matted fur.

"Don't get upset, Two Bums. This is our friend Cas and he's come to spend the evening with us."

Cas couldn't help but smile. "What's his name?"

"Two Bums. He was a stray—still is really, but he visits every day. He's kind of adopted me as his daddy."

"It's an odd name for a cat. Is it from a book?"

"No, no. It's because he has two bums—look." He held the cat's tail in the air and turned its rear to face Cas.

"Yes. I erm ... I see what you mean, but perhaps it's a female cat."

"You aren't as educated as I thought, Cas. Surely you are aware that black and white cats are always male. The same as ginger cats. Tortoiseshells and tabbies are always female."

For a second, Cas doubted his own intelligence, but he remembered his mother's neighbour had a black and white cat and it was definitely female. He'd seen the kittens. Not wanting to contradict Bob, he pulled an 'oh yeah, silly me' face and took a sip of his wine which wiped the look off his face immediately and replaced it with one of a child eating a lemon.

"Is the wine not of your liking?" Bob asked.

"No. It's fine. It's very powerful and I wasn't expecting it. It's good - really good."

Continuing to stroke the cat in a seductive manner, Bob began questioning Cas about his life. Cas watched the man's mouth moving slower and slower. The room looked cloudy with a yellow tint and a buzzing in his ears made it hard to pick out the soft, spoken words that seemed to make no sense. He was drinking the wine at a speed that only lager should be drank at and he wondered what percentage it must be to have such an effect on him so quickly. His eyes drooped and the glass fell from his hand, but he could do nothing. He couldn't move. The yellowness took over his sight getting darker and then blackness engulfed him.

His hearing returned first. Leonard Cohen was blasting out of some speakers somewhere to his right. Cas tried to focus on a moving pink blob in the distance. He couldn't make it out, so attempted something nearer. Looking down at his hands, he saw they were tied to the arms of the chair with duct tape. Raising his head, his vision slowly became clearer.

"What the fuck!"

Bob was completely naked apart from a Batman mask, but there was no mistaking it was him. He was standing on his armchair dancing in a fashion Cas had never seen before. Then he stopped, pointed at Cas and jumped onto the floor like it was part of the dance routine.

"Ha ha! You awaken slightly. Now we can play games. First you tell me why you're here. Are you a spy?"

Cas didn't answer. He wondered if he'd fallen asleep and was having a nightmare, but the last place he could recall being was in that chair and one glass of wine wouldn't have put even him to sleep. He searched the room for a clock. Spotting one that read ten thirty, his brain was even more confused. He must have been out for four hours. He dreaded the thought of what Bob might have been doing in that time. Looking down at his own clothing, it didn't seem to have been tampered with.

Bob danced towards him, his voice getting louder.

"Well! Tell me the truth, Boy."

Realising he was in no position to argue or lie, Cas blurted out. "I want to know where the Krankies live. That's all. I'm not a spy and I don't understand why you think I am."

"No one ever speaks to me, especially in the pub. People generally avoid me, yet you—you buy me a beer, put on my favourite music, sit with me and listen to me, and you show far too much interest in me for my liking. Tell me the truth this time."

"Bob, please. I am telling you the truth. I wish I could think of what you want me to say, but it's really as simple as that. I wanted the Krankies address. I have no ulterior motive. You seemed like an okay kinda guy to me. Please do the right thing and untie me."

Bob snatched a piece of paper up from the table; he returned to his dancing waving the paper like a handkerchief.

"I can't. Not yet. I've got the address right here. Now what do I get in return for it? And call me Sir!"

Cas's mobile rang, but he had no way of reaching it.

"I don't know, Sir, but can I answer that? It might be important."

The music stopped and a repetitive scratching and jumping of an old record player needle brought an air of doom to Cas's ears.

Bob walked right up to his face. Not used to seeing men of that age naked Cas grimaced as the small alien body put its hands on his knees. He tried to kick out, but his legs were also bound.

"Listen, Boy. You are here for my own entertainment. You entertain me and I'll give you this address and let you use your phone."

"What do you want me to do?"

"I want you to dance with me naked. I haven't danced with anyone naked since my wife died and a corpse isn't the best of dancers."

Something about the way that he'd phrased that

sentence sent a fearful shudder through Cas's body. He remembered Lexy saying that Bob had once been married and she didn't know what had happened to the woman. Maybe Bob had murdered his wife and if he was capable of that then Cas's own life could be in danger. He had no choice but to agree.

"Okay! Whatever you want, but you'll have to untie me for me to get naked."

"And let you overpower me and run away? I don't think so."

Bob put the needle at the beginning of the record and the music started again. He left the room and came back with another glass of wine. Holding it to Cas's lips he said, "Drink. Go on, drink it and I'll know you mean it."

"No! It's drugged. I'm not stupid."

"Nor am I and you won't be running. Drink it. When you wake up you'll be naked, but still tied. Then we will dance."

Cas spluttered, trying not to swallow a drop as the wine was poured into his mouth. It was no use. If he didn't swallow, he'd choke to death. Some of it went down. He knew what the effects would be, so he pretended to go into a drowsy sleep, hoping to be untied before the drug really kicked in.

Once his eyes were shut, Bob put the address on Cas's lap, knelt down on the floor and started untying his feet. Opening one eye, Cas read the address. Closing it again, he recited it over in his head. He thought he could hear knocking, but the music drowned out everything. He guessed it was the drug doing something to his brain, but the knocking turned to crashing and as the tune ended a loud smash echoed throughout the house. Bob jumped up and spun around.

Through his now hazy vision, Cas could see Yahoo

marching across the room towards him. He threw Bob to one side.

"What the fuck do you think you're doing?"

Bob landed in his armchair and huddled in the corner.

"It's not my fault. It was the die. The die made me do it. I was planning on making a spaghetti bolonese, but I couldn't make my mind up about the wine. Then it all got out of hand. The die said I had to get him to dance naked with me. I'm sorry. I didn't mean any harm."

While untying Cas's arms, Yahoo screamed back at the man.

"The die didn't make you do it. You chose the options. You were probably thrilled when the die fell on this one. You're a sick bastard and I'm calling the police."

"No! Please don't I haven't done anything wrong. He'll be okay. The die is there on the table. Take it with you. I promise I'll never use it again. Don't get me in trouble. I've never been in trouble in all my life."

Yahoo pulled Cas to his feet, but they weren't having it. He was still conscious, but his body was jelly. Hoisting him over his shoulder, Yahoo grabbed the die from the table before marching out of the house.

"We'll see what Cas has to say about it in the morning. I have no idea what you've done to him yet, but it sure wasn't pretty.

Cas felt the night air hit his face seconds before it all went black again.

Chase

Cas was awoken the next morning by a tap on the cheek from Yahoo. He sat up and blinked at his surroundings.

"Thank God. I had this horrible nightmare."

Shaking his head, Yahoo passed him a cup of sugary tea.

"I'm afraid it wasn't a nightmare, Mate. I was there. What the hell was going on?"

"I don't know. One minute I was all welcome and drinking wine—the next I was tied to a chair and Bob was dancing in the nude. Then you appeared and I don't remember anything after that."

"Well, I put you to bed, but don't worry you still have your boxers on. I called you a couple of times last night, as it was getting late, and when you didn't answer I knew something was up. Lucky, I turned up when I did. Do you think we should call the police? He did drug you after all."

Thinking hard, Cas shook his head.

"What would I tell them? I went round his house for dinner and he went all naked on me and drugged me?"

"Yes. If that's what happened. He might do it to someone else. Who knows what might have happened if I hadn't turned up when I did."

Although Cas knew he was right, he really didn't want to have to explain it all to the police. Surely, they'd find it hilarious and also question what his relationship with Bob was. He'd have to tell them that he'd met him in a pub and accepted an invite for dinner. It just wouldn't seem right.

"Can't we go round there and warn him? You know, just threaten him that we will go to the police if he does anything like it again."

"If that's how you want it, I'll pop round myself now. He did beg with me last night and said he'd never been in trouble before. He blamed a die for the whole thing. I told you that book was dangerous."

"Well, I certainly won't be reading it if that's what it can do to a man. Go round there then—I think that would be best for now. I don't feel up to it myself right now though. My head is spinning, I feel like shit and I didn't even have a good time."

"No worries. You sort yourself out and I'll go and have a word. I won't be long. Shame you didn't video it all. By the way, I washed all the makeup off your face, but it'll take a while for your eyebrows to grow back," Yahoo said laughing and leaving the room.

Cas got up and looked in the mirror. His face was still stained and Yahoo hadn't been joking about the eyebrows.

After a good shower, Cas wrote down the address he'd memorised.

He muttered to himself, "This had better be worth it."

Yahoo was back in no time and looking resigned, but glum.

"He weren't in. A neighbour told me he was taken away at around three in the morning in an ambulance. He'd threatened to kill himself by jumping out the window, so I guess they took him to the loony bin. There should be a warning on that book."

"It is fascinating though that a book is capable of sending people mad."

A smile crept across Yahoo's face. "It depends on the person. It can have a positive effect. You don't find out either way until you've read it though. Anyhow, I've got work to do, Mate. Are you sure you're alright now?"

"Yeah! A black coffee and I'll be fine, I'm sure. I was gonna try and get that scooter started up, if that's okay?"

"Sure. I'll get you the keys and the fob for the garage. Are you planning on going somewhere nice? Off to visit Bob, are we?"

Cas gave him a jab on the arm.

"No! Let's just say that your super-sense might be rubbing off on me. There's something I need to check out."

Yahoo jabbed back.

"That's what I like to hear. Have you got a driving license?"

"No, but I've got a provisional. I can ride a scooter."

"Have you ever ridden one, though? They aren't the best balanced little beasts."

"I'll be sound. Don't worry."

Yahoo gave him the keys and went to his office.

Cas put the address in his pocket and gave himself an imaginary slap on the back. It hadn't been the nicest of experiences to get the info he required, but he had got step one of his plan out of the way. The rest of his mission would be child's play. He left the flat with a spring in his step.

The garage gate opened automatically and Cas was amazed by the size of it. It was almost as big as the flat. The design of this place was cleverly aimed at the rich market. This was a garage for someone with at least four cars. Maybe that was Yahoo's plan in the long run, for now he only had one car and Cas stared longingly at it.

"One day, Baby. One day."

Imagining his own car parked beside it, he smiled to

himself. It wouldn't be something he thought possible a week ago, but Yahoo had shown him that it could be done, even without qualifications or experience.

Finding the old Vespa in a corner covered in dust and cobwebs, he brushed her down and tried to start her. The engine kicked in immediately and filled the garage with thick black fumes. Coughing and spluttering he turned her off and started pushing her outside before attempting anything else. Standing in the middle of the gateway was Two Bums. She mooed at him and he stopped in his tracks. Flashbacks of the night before haunted his brain and the cat became an obstacle between him and his mission. There was something evil about that cat, but he was determined that nothing was going to get in his way today.

He told himself, 'It's just a cat.'

Moving forward to the left, he hissed as he passed it.

"Piss off. Go on, scat you evil creature."

Two Bums came closer until she was winding between his legs. The scooter was a lot heavier than he'd expected, so he couldn't brush her away. He hissed again at the animal until he could stand the scooter on the pavement and gently nudged Two Bums away with his foot.

"Piss off or I'll kick you into next week."

A woman with a pushchair gave him a filthy look and crossed over the road. She leant down to the child and said loudly enough for Cas to hear, "That's a nasty man. Someone should kick him."

The child waved his fist and shouted, "Yeah! Nasty man."

Cas held his arms up trying to look as innocent as possible.

"Don't be trying to fool me. I saw the state you were in—being carried home last night. This is a nice neighbourhood. We don't want your type round here. I don't want my kids growing up thinking your kind of behaviour is normal." She was really going for him.

The kid called out again, "Yeah."

There wasn't much Cas could do or say, but he was now very aware of what his neighbours thought of him.

With the woman out of earshot and Two Bums making all the more effort to annoy him, he closed the garage, unstrapped the helmet and put it on before starting the Vespa up again and weaving off up the road followed by a thick trail of smoke. He knew it was reckless, not to check her over first, but he had to get away from that cat.

Stopping to ask for directions eight times, he realised that the people of the town had either a warped sense of humour or no sense of direction at all. Three of them sent him back to where he'd already been, four of them guided him to one-way streets or cul-de-sacs and one sent him to a vehicle reclamation yard. He stopped at a shop and bought a map.

It was hard trying to control the scooter while reading a map, but he finally reached his destination. He pulled up outside what he hoped was the Krankies' house. He had no reason to think that Bob had lied to him, but the way his luck was, he wasn't taking anything for granted.

The entrance to the drive was gated, but he could see a silver Mini Coupe with a red roof parked in front of the building. Sadly the angle of the car made it impossible for him to see the registration, but it was such a distinct car that he wouldn't have a problem spotting it from miles away. He was thrilled to have got another step closer to mission accomplished in such a short time.

All he had to do now was to find a place he could keep watch and get confirmation that it was indeed their car. Not wanting to look like a stalker, he rode off up the street finding a small row of shops. He parked up the scooter and bought a newspaper before he found himself a seat by the window in a café.

Seventeen cups of coffee, two crosswords and a very welcome egg and chips later, the silver Mini Coupe whizzed past the café. He tried to get a glimpse of the occupants, but the windows of the car were small and tinted.

Leaping from his seat and pulling on his helmet, he ran through the door almost literally, and as he kicked the scooter forward and started her up she exploded into life with an almighty bang.

Swerving from one side of the road to the other, Cas struggled to take full control of the machine. He needed speed to catch that car and even if it wasn't going to a dogging site, he had to get a look at the driver to know that it was The Krankies' car and not just some visitor they'd had. It crossed his mind that they might be going dogging right now. If that was the case, then he could complete his mission today and would never see the inside of the BEET office ever again.

Focusing only on the roof of the car way ahead of him, he didn't spot the road sign warning of a roundabout ahead. The Mini turned right and out of view. His intentions were to do the same, but hitting the small roundabout at high speed caused him to lose any control he had over the Vespa. On a collision course with a tarmac truck, he struggled to steer the zigzagging scooter out of danger. Losing his balance, the machine skidded along the ground on its side crashing into a bollard. He tumbled across the road and when he finally stopped, he expected something to hit him and was frozen with fright. The truck tried to avoid him and braked hard. Cas watched in slow motion as it approached, skidded and stopped inches from his body. A curly-ginger-haired man fell from the passenger door and tumbled towards him.

Totally stunned by his close shave, Cas lay there and watched the ginger guy sit bolt upright and shake his mop of hair before crawling up next to him and tugging at his helmet until he'd yanked it right off. He peered down at Cas's face and frowned.

"Mate, are you okay?"

Cas was winded and struggled to make a sound. The ginger man took a half bottle of whisky from his inside pocket, unscrewed the lid and lifted Cas's head up off the road.

"This'll do you good. You're in shock, Mate. All your eyebrow hairs have fell out and I don't mind sharing it with you," he said, as he started pouring the liquor down Cas's throat.

After his experience yesterday of almost drowning, he swallowed it down without a struggle.

The driver of the truck marched over and snatched the bottle from the ginger guy and started shouting at him.

"Joe, you daft bugger. What do you think you're doing?"

"He's in shock. It's the best thing for him."

"It'll put him in gaol, you fool! Sometimes you are so thick."

"Don't call me thick," Joe shouted back.

"Why not? You are thick. I've rung an ambulance and they said not to remove his helmet. I know not to remove his helmet, but ... too late. Thicko has pulled his helmet off."

"I said don't call me thick." Joe rose to his feet.

"Thick, thick, thick, thick, thick," the driver screamed in his face.

Joe swung the first punch and Cas closed his eyes as the two men partook in a full-on fistfight over his trembling body. A siren in the distant paused the fighting.

Cas opened his eyes to see the driver pointing at the truck with one hand while gripping Joe's neck with the other.

"Get back in the truck. I'll wait with him until they arrive and tell them that some idiot had already removed his helmet."

"You can call me an idiot, but don't ever call me thick, okay?"

"Okay." He released his grip and Joe staggered off back to the truck.

The driver moved the scooter to the pavement and guided the traffic, so as not to have Cas run over as well.

With the build-up of traffic on the road, it took an age for the ambulance to arrive and the police beat them to the scene.

A mean-looking constable strutted over, knelt down and peered into Cas's eyes. He held up a finger pushing it right up to Cas's nose and slowly away again. Then he bent over and sniffed his face.

"What happened?"

"I swerved and lost my balance."

"Have you been drinking?"

"Only tea."

"Smells like strong tea to me."

"You don't understand. I was given the drink after I crashed. There wasn't a drop in me before it happened. Ask ..." Cas sat up and pointed to where the truck had been, but it was gone.

"A likely story. Is that your scooter?"

"No. It's my flatmate's."

"So, I guess you have no insurance either. A license even?"

"I have a license, Officer, but no, I don't have any

insurance."

"The license should spare you a few months off your prison term, but you'll definitely be going down. We'll escort you to the hospital and breathalyse you there."

"But I haven't done anything wrong."

"Drink driving, reckless driving, driving without insurance—I might even find something else to add if you fancy trying to resist arrest."

"I'm not resisting anything. I promise, but what about the scooter? I can't leave it here."

"We'll be impounding that. Your mate will have to prove it's his and pay the fine to get it back. You'd better get in that ambulance, Pretty boy."

Two men put a stretcher down next to him and asked him if anything hurt.

He shook his head, not caring if anything hurt or not. The thought of being sent to prison and never being able to complete his mission made him believe that fate truly had it in for him.

As he lay in the ambulance, on the way to the hospital, he figured that there was only so much luck in the world and Yahoo was hogging more than his fair share of it, leaving him with only the bad luck. His life had gone downhill since he'd moved in with Yahoo and under different circumstances he would have decided to move out. He had no choice in the matter now. He was going to gaol.

At the hospital the policeman pounced on him before they'd even got him through the doors. The breathalyser confirmed that he was over the limit to drive and they arrested him.

After a few tests, he was given the all clear by the doctors. His ankle was badly bruised and swollen, but he could just about manage to hobble to the police car.

He was taken to the police station where he was charged with drink driving, reckless driving and having no insurance. No one mentioned resisting arrest to his relief.

"Do you want to call your solicitor or someone that might be worried about you?" the young policewoman at the desk asked.

"I don't have a solicitor. I've never been a criminal before, but I'd like to ring my flatmate and tell him where I am."

"Go ahead. Then we'll lock you up until someone has the time to interview you."

Taking out his phone with great resentment, he called the guy who he was blaming all his misfortune on.

"Yahoo! Hi. I ... well ... something's happened."

"I know, Mate. Don't worry. Where are you?"

"The police station."

"Give me an hour or two and I'll get you out of there." He hung up.

Cas was confused by Yahoo's calmness and awareness. He had sounded like some Mafia guy on the phone and it wasn't at all the response he'd expected. Then he was stripped of his belongings, including his phone, belt and boots and locked in a cell.

With nothing at all to do, the next two hours were worse than a whole day in the BEET office. He couldn't imagine how he'd stay sane in a prison for months. The only glimmer of hope was that Yahoo really would have some kind of influence over these policemen. His mind started wandering about what it could be. Maybe Yahoo had videos that he could bribe the police with. It wouldn't surprise him at all. Shaking himself back to his doubting reality, it seemed more likely that Yahoo didn't realise the full extent of what had happened and would be of no help to him at all.

Then the regrets began. If he'd only driven more carefully, where could he be now? The Krankies were probably dogging away for all to see at that very moment and where was he? Imprisoned and for how long, he didn't know.

The hatch on the door opened revealing the policewoman's face.

"You decent?" she said.

"Yes. Of course I'm decent." He couldn't imagine what she meant by that.

The door was opened and she gestured with a thumb swing.

"Get your stuff from the desk and you can go."

Cas limped behind, trying to keep up with her, to the front desk where Yahoo was waiting.

The woman handed him a plastic bag containing his belongings and a sheet of paper.

"Check it, sign for it and heed this as a warning. If we catch you doing anything remotely out of order, you won't be so lucky next time. You'll be going down for a long stretch—got that?"

"Yes, Officer. I understand. Thank you, Officer."

"Don't thank me. I'm not doing you any favours. Thank your buddy."

"Okay and thanks again." Cas signed the sheet, slipped on his boots painfully and grabbed his things not even bothering to mess with his belt. He wanted to get out of the place, but was still flabbergasted that he was free to go and wary that they might change their minds. He hopped out of the station on one leg.

A taxi was sitting outside.

"I had to get a cab cos someone took the garage key with them and I couldn't find the spare one."

"I'm sorry. I didn't think. I'll pay for it."

As they walked to a taxi, Cas didn't know which question to ask first. He kept looking around at the outside world and thinking how close he'd come to losing his freedom. Then he looked at Yahoo who seemed totally unfazed by the situation and had a pang of guilt for how he'd blamed him for his misfortune earlier. The guy wasn't that bad at all; he'd just saved his life.

Eventually coming to his wits and finding his tongue, Cas questioned Yahoo on the drive home.

"I don't understand why they let me go. What just happened? The policeman said I'd go to prison for this and for a long time—then you turn up and everything's fine and I'm set free."

"Sorted, Mate. You got a warning."

"But why? He was insistent that he was putting me down. He was even going to make up other charges to make sure of it."

"There are many aspects to it, Cas."

"Please enlighten me, Oh-mighty-one. I'm beginning to think you are some kind of God."

"Maybe I'll let you think that."

Cas elbowed Yahoo. "Come on. How did you even know something had happened and why have I been let off?"

"First off. The minute you left the flat, I added you to my insurance details—for my own peace of mind. Lucky for you that I did—that was one charge dropped as soon as I proved it. Anyway, I was going to pop out on a hunch, but you'd took the garage fob with you. I went down there on the off chance that you'd left it open. You hadn't and I couldn't get to my car. I was a little peeved, but then I saw this strange black and white cat. It was bellowing at me like a bull, so I started filming it. I went back to the flat and edited the footage with me having a conversation with the creature in a Postman Pat accent. You couldn't see me of course, but I created a great sketch consisting of Pat telling Jes the cat that she was having a personality crisis and however much she believed she was a cow, she would always look like a cat. It went on with talk of psychiatrists and the cat protesting with moos. It turned out really funny and I made a shorter video of it too—with captions. I put both on the internet and within a few hours the small one had gone viral and the long one was getting the views that I'm used to. I couldn't be upset that you'd taken the garage keys after that. I'll show you it when we get back."

"What has that got to do with me being released?"

"Well, while I was online, this fan sends me an email saying that he's got some footage and would I like to buy it from him or could I edit it for him. I told him I'd need to see it first. Guess who it was of?"

"Me! Crashing your scooter?"

"It was indeed. I was a little mad at first, but I watched it all and saw what that fella did to you—pouring whiskey down your throat. I said I'd buy it for fifty quid and the guy accepted. Then you called me. That's how I knew what had happened. I transferred it to a stick and took it with me to the police station where I insisted they watch it and that you'd be using it as evidence if it went to court. You would clearly be let off the drink driving charge, so they would be wasting their time holding you. So, you were insured, you had a licence, you weren't drink driving and the reckless driving was due to your lack of experience on a scooter rather than having a drunken, reckless mind. As you have no previous convictions, they couldn't do much else other than give you a warning. I guess I'm not such a God now."

"No. It's still bloody impressive, though."

"If I was in your shoes, I think I'd have preferred prison, as now you owe me fifty quid for the video, fifty quid for a taxi there and back and the charge for getting my scooter out of the pound. Did you get what you were after today? Do you think it'll cover it?"

"I'll give you the money when I get my first wage slip and I didn't get what I went for, but I will tomorrow if you'll let me borrow the scooter again. I'll be more careful—I promise."

"Sure you can if you've got a hunch that you think'll pay off. We'll pick it up in the morning. And I'm only teasing about the money. Pay me back when you can. I'll probably make a bit out of those two guys fighting over the top of your body in the middle of the roundabout. Don't look horrified, you can't see your face on that part. The guy shooting it was more interested in the fight by then than your wellbeing. You have to be the unluckiest person I've ever met. "

"And you, the luckiest."

Yahoo leaned forward to the driver. "Could you drop us at The White Horse, please? I think this man needs a drink and so do I. That was a long day."

They arrived at the pub ten minutes before regular closing hours.

Cas hobbled across the room to the bar while Yahoo paid the driver.

"Two pints, please. He's just coming."

Lexy stood staring at him with her hands on her hips. It kind of reminded him of how his mother looked when he came home injured as a small boy. She'd look mad with him and then she'd fix him and pamper him. Yahoo walked in and Cas realised his interpretation of her stance had been way off course.

Shouting at the pair of them, Lexy held up her arms.

"What time do you call this? You two waltzing and limping in here and expecting me to serve you 'til the early hours. You're taking the piss now, boys."

Yahoo held up his palm.

"Give us a break, Girl. If you knew the day this man had had, you'd be buying him a drink. What's up with you anyway? That crazy boyfriend been giving you shit again?"

She started pouring the beer with a shaking hand.

"No. I've hardly seen him lately."

As soon as Cas opened his mouth, he wished he hadn't. "I've never seen him."

"That's because he's barred from here. In fact, he's barred from every pub in the town and my personal life is none of your concern. What's wrong with your face? There's something odd about it."

"Sorry I spoke," Cas said, looking into the mirror behind her and being reminded he had no eyebrows. He shrugged not wanting to discuss where they'd gone.

Yahoo patted Cas on the shoulder. "Don't be afraid of her. She's a woman and they get like this sometimes."

Slamming the glasses down in front of them both she screamed, "Have 'em. Have 'em for your shite day. Don't worry about me."

"Whoa! What's happened to you then?" Yahoo asked, seeing that his 'woman' joke hadn't helped matters.

"Him upstairs—he's gone. I went up earlier to get some change for the till and the safe was empty. All his personal stuff is gone and the cellar has been cleared of every bottle of spirit. There's a dice and Bob's book left on the coffee table in the lounge. That's it, no note, no explanation, nothing. I tried ringing the area manager, but got an answer machine saying the office is closed 'til Monday morning. I don't know what to do."

"I think we should have a party."

"Yahoo, that's not funny. This is my job at stake."

"Okay. Carry on as usual and ring the office on

Monday. It seems you don't have much choice. Take your wages out of the takings."

"Oh, yeah. That's a great idea until Monday. Then what? It'll be another shut down, boarded up pub and I'm out of a job."

"Not necessarily. They might put someone else in to run it."

"And they'll want to run it themselves, their way. I won't get the hours I got with him if they want me at all."

"Tell the area manager that you want to run it then."

"Don't be stupid. I'm just a barmaid. Anyway it's not a managed pub it's a leasehold. A lease costs money and I don't have any."

"I can't think of anyone better qualified and experienced as you to run this place and if they're desperate for a new tenant—they might do you a good deal."

"You're talking shit. They wouldn't even think about it."

"Don't tell me I'm talking shit until you've given it a go and can prove I'm talking shit."

Although Cas couldn't bring himself to speak to either of them the way they were bickering at each other, he managed to smile and nod in agreement at both of them in turn.

Lexy's face softened as she looked up at the clock.

"I have to close the doors, lads. We'll have a drink and you can tell me why Cas is limping and has no eyebrows."

Chips

The following morning Cas and Yahoo set off to the pound in the Audi TT with the roof down. Cas was dying to ask how much the car had cost, but he didn't think he should. Trying to tone down how impressed he was by it, he chatted away as if he was quite used to travelling in such luxury.

"I saw that cat you videoed yesterday. I can't believe I didn't think to do the same. I shooed it away, got accused of being an evil man by one of the neighbours and her kid and then the rest of the day went completely pear-shaped. Whereas you saw the damn creature and made money out of the situation."

"You had the feeling, though, and you didn't recognise it when it was staring you in the face. You'll get the hang of it eventually."

"I need to get the hang of the scooter too. Why would anyone design something so difficult to steer?"

"It's about style, Cas. It's a look—it's not made to be flung wildly around corners. Stay cool and it'll treat you right. You'll get the hang of it if you haven't killed it."

It was a beautiful day with a clear blue sky and the slight breeze was warm against Cas's skin. The tranquillity was broken by a white streak in the sky that grew bigger and brighter before exploding into a huge fire ball. All the traffic stopped and a fantastic boom sent shock waves that shook everything around. Then everything went back to how it was and all that remained was a white scar in the sky that began to disperse and fade.

"Did you see that?" Cas yelled.

"Oh, yes. What a beauty. How could I miss it?"

"What the hell was it?"

"I'd say it was a comet or a meteor. Nothing to worry about." Yahoo parked the car at the side of the road.

"Damn it, Yahoo. I didn't even get the chance to pick my phone up."

Reaching to the dash board, Yahoo patted a small device attached to it.

"This little chap did. I have to get it to the news channels and upload it on my site. It shouldn't take me long."

He fiddled with the dash cam and spent a while on his mobile. Cas wondered why things didn't fall into his lap the way they seemed to with Yahoo. He decided to try harder, to be more aware of the things around him, to get out more and to remember to always have his phone in his hand with his thumb on the button. He knew that wasn't going to be easy stuck in the BEET office all week, so he had to make the most of what little time he had. It crossed his mind to take up smoking, so he could at least get his mobile from security several times a day and await a happening in the smoking area. He chose against the idea at the thought of being accosted by Bendy Wendy every time he left the building.

Starting the car up, Yahoo gave a big grin. "I'm done. That was the easiest money I think I've ever earned. I didn't even have to edit it—they bought it how it was."

"Your luck honestly amazes me. If I didn't know you for real and had only heard about you, I'd believe you are a Jedi knight from a fictional world."

"I was a boy scout for a while. Be prepared—that's the

only bit I remember, but it serves me well."

When they reached the pound, Yahoo checked over the scooter.

"It's a bit scuffed, but you haven't killed her off yet. I'll get her touched up during the week. She could do with a new paint job—I've neglected the old girl in the last few years. Do you think you can drive her home a little slower and try getting the hang of cornering?"

Cas nodded. "I promise I'll be really careful with her."

"I'll add the repairs and the pound charge to your bill," Yahoo said, as he paid for the release of his injured Vespa.

Cas put on the helmet and started her up, and the black smoke belched from her exhaust.

"I'll see you back home," he called out, as he weaved off.

At the gates of the pound, Cas indicated to go left and waited, as the silver Mini Coupe passed right in front of him going in the opposite direction. Believing it to be a sign, and for once he was in the right place at the right time, he turned right and followed the car at a reasonable speed.

The traffic lights were good to him. Whenever the Mini got almost out of view, the lights would turn red and give Cas the chance to catch up. He reckoned that if the dogging spot was out of town and they got onto country roads that he would probably lose them due to his lack of power. He would have an idea of where he was heading though and the car wouldn't be hard to miss if he searched the area. He was hopeful he'd find the spot.

The silver Mini turned off the main road and into a large supermarket car park. Cas stopped at the entrance, not wanting to be spotted tailing them. The car parked up and to Cas's sheer delight, he watched as The Krankies got out. He punched his fist in the air.

"Yes! You little beauty." The next step of his mission was complete. It was The Krankies' car. He ticked an imaginary tick box in his mind.

They didn't look like he'd expected. The wife wasn't dressed as a school boy to start with, but he could tell by their statures that it was definitely them. He watched them cross the car park, collect a trolley and go into the store like any normal couple would. Then he waited. It dawned on him that they might merely be going shopping and would travel straight home. He convinced himself otherwise, as luck was on his side today. If they were true avid doggers, and were out for the day in their car, then they'd probably go to the spot and do their stuff at some point. All he had to do was stay calm, drive carefully and he'd catch the moment and be on his way to being a very wealthy man.

Watching the shop front, he didn't see them leave the supermarket. He was looking out for a couple to exit the huge revolving glass door. It was only when he flicked his gaze back to the car, to check it was still there, that he noticed it pulling out of the parking space. The wife must have been hidden by the trolley loaded with goods. He was flustered for a moment, but took a deep breath and told himself everything would be fine if he stayed calm. On the turn of the key, the scooter spluttered and died. He panicked and tried it again, but nothing. The fuel gauge was showing the tank was half full until he tapped it hard. Slowly, the needle fell to empty. The silver Mini Coupe passed him by, as he stepped down and began to push the hungry Vespa, very tentatively on his sore ankle, to the store's petrol station.

For once the scooter hadn't backfired, but his plan had. He filled her up and had one hope left. He guessed they might have bought some frozen food and they'd probably go home and drop it off first. He could make up ground while they unloaded the shopping and follow them again later. It was wishful thinking and a long shot, but even with his small disaster, of running out of petrol, he had a sense that today fate was on his side and he would succeed in his mission. He had to, otherwise, tomorrow he would be back in the BEET office, trapped for maybe another week of agony before he got the chance again.

He drove off in the direction of The Krankies' house remembering exactly how to find it because he'd become much more aware of his surroundings, thanks to Yahoo. Even his skills controlling the scooter were improving with every corner he carefully navigated, as his confidence grew that his plan was soon to result in success.

Reaching the gates of The Krankies' driveway, he peered through them, but could see no sign of their vehicle. The café was closed, so he waited across the street and tinkered with the scooter, as if he was fixing something, until late in the afternoon when it began to rain hard. His mood dropped and all he could do was stand there and imagine what The Krankies were up to for all to see, except him.

Once he was soaked through to the bone, he gave up. He realised he was wasting his time hanging around there and waiting for the chase. What he needed to do, was to get some local knowledge of the area. Surely if he broached the subject the right way, someone would tell him where the dogging spots were. At least then, he could place himself in the right place and hope that he'd got the right time and they would come to him. It was impossible to ask Yahoo. He'd be bound to catch on to what he was up to. He'd realise what a fantastic opportunity it was and take on the challenge himself. Knowing Yahoo's luck The Krankies would turn up right outside his flat and start dogging with all the lights on, at the same second that Yahoo was taking the bins out with his mobile in his hand. The reality of that scenario was almost enough to make Cas cry.

Asking at work was a no-no too. He didn't know anyone there all that well and they might get the wrong idea and spread it around that he was weirdo. He already had a bad reputation with his neighbours and he didn't fancy women walking down the street and pointing him out to their children as some kind of pervert to steer clear of. Wendy was definitely out of bounds. She would get the wrong idea and offer to take him out there. He didn't bear to think where that would lead.

Riding home, he pondered on his dilemma. The only person he could think of to ask was Lexy, but he had to phrase it right. If she got the wrong impression, she might tell her boyfriend that he was coming onto her in a creepy way and he didn't fancy another trip to the hospital or one to the cemetery.

As he came up with the perfect solution to question her, he recalled what she'd said the night before about the Landlord. She might be gone already and he didn't know where she lived. The pub could be being boarded up right there and then like all the others in the area. Instead of going home and getting into some dry clothes, he went straight to The White Horse to see what was happening and if she was still around.

Turning into the street, he was relieved to see the place looking normal. The windows were still glass and as he pulled up alongside, the outer door was open.

He parked up and went inside.

Lexy poured his beer, as he limped across the room leaving puddle tracks.

"Have you been swimming today, Cas?" she asked.

"No. It's raining."

"I know you have a bad ankle, but it must have taken you a hell of a long time to walk here to get that wet."

"I didn't walk here. I've been out getting to know my way around town and my way around Yahoo's dodgy scooter."

"Did you find anywhere nice?"

"Strangely, I didn't. The place is quite a dump. I was thinking of going for a ride out of the town, but it started chucking it down with rain, so I turned back."

"Well, make sure you avoid the reservoir car park. There are strange goings-on there. If you want to see the reservoir, carry on past the car park sign until you see the trout fishing sign and park up there."

"What kind of strange goings-on?"

Lexy leant over the bar, placed his pint in front of him and whispered, "Doggers!"

Realising his face had lit up, he forced his expression down into a look of disgust.

She took his money and went off to serve someone else.

Cas was stunned how easy it was to get the information he'd wanted. He hadn't even tried to get it out of her. All the long-winded ideas he'd had about bringing up the subject were washed from his brain. He was even slightly disappointed that he hadn't got to use them, but he was elated that he was another step closer to mission accomplished. He was learning, but he was learning the hard way. Everything he did was the wrong way round. The answers were out there, ready and waiting for him, but he wasn't very good at the way he went about getting them. Thinking about Yahoo's approach, he realised how little the guy tried and that was where he himself was failing. He'd wasted a day outside of a supermarket and in a street getting drowned because he'd thought too much. Lexy could have told him yesterday about the reservoir car park if he'd had the same conversation then, and he could have gone straight there today and waited for them to come to him, but his mind had been set on his plan and taken him away from a vital piece of information. He decided that from then on he wouldn't push his mind to concoct hair-brained schemes, but leave it more to his instincts if he could find them. He had the information he needed now, so the next part of the plan should be relatively easy.

Sipping at his beer, he drifted off into a little dream world. He could see the future and the views number clocking up. He could see his new car parked next to Yahoo's and his mother's proud face. Then his mother's mad face and her slamming her front door in his when she found out how he came about the money.

He was jolted out of his trance by Lexy.

"Cas!"

"Sorry. What? I did pay you, didn't I?"

"You did, but you're away with fairies. Is it the thought of the weird things that go on in this strange town?"

"Not at all. We have that kind of pervy stuff going on in my town too. I was just thinking about what you said last night. Did the Landlord come back?"

"No, he didn't and I thought sod it. Yahoo was right. I should carry on as normal and take my wages from the till. I'll ring the area manager tomorrow and explain what's happened. It might look good for me if they see I've kept the cogs turning and the beer flowing since I've been left on my own. I went to the wholesalers this morning and stocked up on spirits with the takings. The worst that can happen is they sack me and the best—that they see I have initiative."

"So you're really thinking of taking it on yourself?"

"Don't be a ninny, but they might put in a good word about me to the new guy. I'm not even thinking about them closing it down. I couldn't bear the thought."

Reaching over, Cas put his hand on top of hers.

"I'm sure it'll all turn out okay for you. They're still taking on new people at the BEET office if you get stuck."

She pulled her hand from under his.

"I'm not surprised. No one lasts more than a week there unless they are mental."

With that, and knowing it was a dig at him because he'd already been there a week, Cas swigged his pint down and got up to leave.

"I've gotta go. I don't want to get done for drink driving again. I might catch you later."

Lexy laughed and waved her hand.

Calling Yahoo on his mobile to open the garage, Cas rode the short distance home and met him at the gate.

Still dripping wet, Cas was faced with a very relieved-looking Yahoo.

"What happened this time, Cas? Don't tell me you rode into the canal."

"No. I just got wet from the rain. Don't worry, she's safely back in one piece."

"I watched you at the pound. You indicated left and then turned right. How on earth did you get a provisional license?"

"It wasn't like that. I was going left to come home—then I had a sense. I turned right instead. It was too late to indicate."

"You have some messed up sense, Cas—unless you have the proof of it on you. Did you get a video?"

"I was following the sense, but I ran out of petrol. You didn't tell me the gauge gets stuck on half full."

Yahoo held his belly and roared with laughter, as he closed the garage and they both walked up to the flat.

"I see you're staying positive, Cas. It's nice to hear you say half full instead of half empty. I can't believe you ran out of petrol. No. I can, you unlucky bugger. You go and get out of those wet things. I saved you some dinner—I'll put it in the microwave."

They walked to separate rooms, but Cas could still hear him chuckling away and repeating what he'd said to himself.

Noticing the flat didn't smell as nice as usual, Cas changed and went warily to the kitchen. He stared at the plate of food on the table.

"What is it?"

"It's beef Sunday roast."

Not wanting to complain, and it made a change from pasta, Cas sat down and tackled the rectangular lump on his plate.

"Where's yours?" he asked.

"In the bin. I don't know what happened. I put the boxes in the oven like it said. The instructions said - cook from frozen and when I got them out, they were like that. I thought you might want to give it a go. It was meant to be a surprise, but it wasn't as easy as I thought."

"I think I'll pass. I don't think you're meant to cook it in the tray and the box. Next Sunday I'll cook you a real roast dinner and you'll enjoy it. It won't consist of any plastic or cardboard, I assure you."

Yahoo clapped his hands.

"Oh, goody that sounds great. You'll have to show me how to do it. If it's not Italian, I don't have a clue."

Dropping the lump in the bin, Cas smiled. "You really don't, do you? Have I spotted a chink in that armour of yours?"

"Nobody's perfect, Mate. Come and see what I got today, because I turned left to come home and not right."

Cas almost had him, but resigned himself to the fact that in a few moments' time he was going to regret turning right out of the pound more than he already did. Standing at the doorway of Yahoo's office was like being on a game show and losing. Cas knew he was about to be shown what he could have won.

Yahoo beckoned him in.

"Come closer. You have to see this—it's mental. I've sent it to the news, but I'm thinking about what to do with the editing for my own record. I need the right tune and I've been searching for hours."

The video began and Yahoo ran through the events.

"So, I was driving home from the pound and I saw this police car and fire engine outside this house. Normally I would have just driven on. If it was a house fire or something distressing for the occupants, they don't want someone filming them and no one really wants to watch stuff like that. It's just cruel and it could be me one day. I like to stick to the funny stuff or things of real headline hitting news interest. I've got my rep to think of you know? I sensed not to drive on, but I didn't start filming immediately. What I did notice was that the street was strangely quiet for this kind of incident. People were looking from the windows of the neighbouring houses, but no one was out in the street. That's when I turned on the camera. I'll fast forward it a bit cos nothing's happening for a while."

It gave Cas the time to reflect on his plan.

"So, how do you know when and where to draw the line on what you would put out there and what you won't?"

Yahoo paused the video.

"I guess you learn what works and what doesn't. If you get bad comments telling you you're sick, it could ruin you. Then again it could cause a mass influx of views. There are people that make sick stuff and people that want to watch it. You need to decide what works for you. I wouldn't want to have to keep reinventing myself because people hated me. What I do is interesting or damn funny and that doesn't seem to upset anyone."

"So, if it's harmless and funny and you haven't spied on anyone without their consent, that would be fine?"

"Sure it would. Now do you want to watch this? I was hoping to pop out for a couple of bevies this evening."

"Go on. Carry on," Cas said, pleased that his plan fitted the criteria.

"Right! So here's the policeman looking through the letter box. He shrugs and the fireman climbs the ladder to the upstairs window. He looks in and I have never seen anyone descend a ladder that quickly. I'll fast forward it and zoom in. Look at the window. That's a polar bear in there. A real, live, fully grown Bloody polar bear. Can you believe it? Someone has had a polar bear as a pet in a terraced house for years—probably since it was a cub. Well, the police and fire brigade all got back in their vehicles and must have rung for assistance. They didn't even get out to warn the pedestrians who were passing by. It took ages for a guy with a tranquiliser gun to turn up. Wait a sec. Look, this is him. He goes up the ladder with a fireman who smashes the window and he shoots the beast, as the ladder is drawn away. There was a horrible sound that can't be appreciated on this recording, but I'll improve that. Anyhow, it soon goes quiet and they go in to get the creature out, but they can't. He's too big for the door or the window. Here's them taking out the front wall of the house and then finally, they get a crane over to lift the sleeping bear out. I asked one of the neighbours for some info on the owner of the house and they said they hadn't seen him for weeks. They'd been hearing a lot of banging, so they called the police to investigate. I bet you any money they never find the guy. They might be able to trace something of him in the shit that bear left behind."

Looking confused, Cas said, "I thought that's the kind of thing that you've just said isn't funny. Isn't that a bit sick to say that the owner is now polar bear poo?"

"I'm not gonna say that on the video. That's just what I think. This is serious—for the news. They pay big money if you're quick enough with the photos, videos and neighbour interviews. They'll edit it themselves for the broadcast. I'm done with it for now, but will make my own unique cut of it. I was going to see what Lexy's planning on doing. I saw the pub was open on my way back, but it looked like it was going to rain, so I put the car away. That's something else you need to learn to sense—the weather. You'll never get good quality footage on a mobile if it's pissing down with rain or you're shivering cos you're soaked to the bone."

"Believe me, I'm learning every hour of the day and you'll have some competition soon," Cas replied.

"Yeah right! I'll worry about it when I see you video something resembling a little more than the inside of your pocket lining. Are you coming out?"

"I'll come for a couple. I saw Lexy earlier and she's hanging in there until she can get in touch with the area manager tomorrow. There was somewhere I wanted to go, but I've been drowned once today, so I'll give it a miss. Like you say - it's not worth it in this rain. I'll get some chips on the way though. I'm starving."

"Good thinking. We should get Lexy something too. She probably hasn't had the chance to eat today."

They went into the bar, sat down and opened up the best pie and chips Cas had smelt in a long time. He pushed a paper bundle across to Lexy, as she gave them their pints.

"I thought you must be starving being stuck here on your own all day, so we bought you some too."

She nodded. "I am ravenous. I had a packet of peanuts this morning before opening up and a packet at lunchtime. I'll get blocked up if I carry on at this rate. There's nothing in the kitchen and I daren't even have a drink on an empty stomach. I can see why the man upstairs turned out how he did though and bunked off out of it. This place would be like a prison if you had to run it on your own."

Yahoo stuffed a handful of chips into his mouth.

"So, you're not thinking of taking it on then? Your boyfriend could help out and you could get staff to do the odd shift."

"One - Did your mother not ever tell you 'not to speak with your mouth full'? Two - I know nothing about running a business. Three - My boyfriend is barred from pubs for a very good reason and if he isn't suitable as a customer, how the hell would he be suitable as a Landlord? Four - I don't have the money. And five - Can you imagine little me being in charge of staff?"

"Yes. Five - I could. You have something scary about you, but you're nice too. Four - You can get a loan. Three - I don't understand why you stay with that thug anyway. Two - If you get an accountant, you don't have to worry about the business side of things. And one - You sound just like my mother. You act like you've got balls, Lexy, so do something with them."

Cas wondered how Yahoo got away with being so cheeky, but so honest. Lexy hadn't shot him down for the statement like she would have done if he'd said it. Keeping his mouth shut while he ate, might make her respect him a little more.

She turned to Cas. "What do you think, Mr. Clumsy? You're very quiet tonight."

Pointing to his mouth, he struggled to swallow the chips down before answering.

"I don't know really. I guess it must be quite hard to be a business person. I found it difficult enough to get a regular job. It never occurred to me that I could work for myself like he does. But then, everything he touches turns to gold."

Yahoo pointed his finger first at Cas and then at Lexy. "If you never touch anything then you haven't a hope in hell of it turning to gold. That's what's wrong with the pair of you. You're too scared to touch."

That made Cas a little mad. He wanted to tell Yahoo about all the trouble he'd gone to in his attempt to capture the most entertaining video ever, but he held his secret plan in. He'd have it soon. Maybe tomorrow evening if the weather was good and then he'd show him what he was capable of.

Lexy was looking very thoughtful though and Cas wondered if Yahoo had struck a nerve with her. He would have liked to encourage her more himself, but he couldn't handle the responsibility of pushing her into something that might go terribly wrong for her and that she'd regret—forever blaming him.

Snapping out of her thoughts, Lexy retaliated. "I'm not scared of anything."

"You could have fooled me," Yahoo continued.

"I'm not scared—it's just ridiculous. I can see them now—they'll laugh in my face if I mention running this place myself."

"You don't know that. Okay, you say you're not scared of anything, but you sound like you're scared of humiliation."

"No. I just don't want to be humiliated."

"Well, don't touch it then. When Cas gets his job at the post office, there'll be a vacancy at the BEET office. I'm sure he could put a word in and I can wrap Wendy around my little finger."

"You will do no such thing. I'd rather shoot myself than do a day in that place."

"So, you'd rather die than be humiliated. Huh, it must really scare you. Pour us another beer and stop making excuses for your chicken brain."

"Yahoo, you are a pig."

"I'd rather be a pig than a chicken."

Cas had heard enough. Not only had he inadvertently been demeaned to the lowest life form by Lexy because of where he worked, but all the talk of chickens reminded him that in a few hours time he'd be entering that airlock for another week of torturous boredom.

"Stop it, the pair of you. I don't want to work in that place as much as you don't. It's the last thing I want to talk about on my day off. I know I have to go there in the morning and you, Lexy, have to ring the area manager and tell him what's happened. There's nothing either of us can do about it right now, so does anyone know any decent jokes that don't involve me?"

Yahoo looked surprised and impressed. "Now, now. Keep your eyebrows on, Son."

Handing them the pints, Lexy had a little chuckle. Even Cas managed to smile as the tension was broken, though the joke was still on him. He held up his pint.

"To tomorrow, and it being a lucky day for all of us."

"To tomorrow," they repeated.

"Now, no more talk of it tonight. Let's put some tunes on and just chill out," Cas said. He was really quite proud of his little outburst.

"Me first." Yahoo headed for the juke box.

"And no Leonard Cohen," Lexy and Cas yelled in unison.

Cas winked at her, though he wasn't very good at it.

"This time next year, we'll be millionaires like him."

"Yeah. I'll race you."

They high-fived each other over the bar.

The Chicken Song started to blare out of the jukebox and they threw the remaining chips at Yahoo.

Something had changed and there was positivity in the air.

Yahoo exposed another hidden talent of his by telling an abundance of chicken jokes that were actually funny. Although Cas was having a great time, he had to be up early, so he finished his pint and said his goodbyes, leaving them to it.

His sleep was filled with chickens which were laughing and rolling around, but they weren't laughing at him, they were laughing at his video on their computer screens. It's amazing what a few beers can do.

Action

As he logged into his workstation and listened to the clucking around him, he wished he could go into some kind of trance to get through the day and back to his mission. All that was left was to find the reservoir car park and wait for the action.

Someone from the night shift must have left a magazine behind next to his computer. He glanced at the headline stories on the cover as he fobbed off the callers. *'I found out my lover was my grandmother.' 'My ex had a sex change to spite me.' 'My wife will only have sex twice a year.'*

Wondering what strange kind of people really wanted to read this stuff, he realised there must be a huge market for it. These were the people who wouldn't be able to resist watching his video over and over and sharing it with all their friends. It would be more popular than anything Yahoo had come up with and it'd be bigger than even he had first imagined. His excitement made him resent the office that trapped him more than it had last week. He answered the phone, then looked at the mag, another caller and he looked back at the mag. Then it hit him, as if one headline story had lit up and flashed at him. His heart sank and every bit of positive energy left his body in that second. Closing his eyes, he bashed his head down onto his keyboard over and over again, but he could still see the flashing line on the back of his eyelids. *'My wife will only *have sex twice a year.'* Knowing that he'd been stupid enough to think that The Krankies went dogging every day, like the way someone might walk their dog, he realised the flaw in his plan. It could take him six months or more to get the footage he so desperately needed. What if they only did it at Christmas or on their anniversary? He'd have to stalk the reservoir car park everyday for the next year and that meant being stuck in this place for a lot longer than he could stand the thought of.

He stopped banging his head on the keyboard and looked around to see if anyone had noticed. Unsurprisingly, no one had batted an eyelid.

A particularly small woman passed by his desk, ignoring him, on her way to welfare-room and an idea struck him. If things didn't go to plan and he didn't capture The Krankies dogging by the end of the week, it could be possible to set something up. Yahoo had set up many videos before he'd learnt to control his sense. There was no reason why Cas couldn't do the same. He could pay a couple of people, actors or someone who really needed the money, to dress up as The Krankies and do their thing. He realised he didn't have the money to spare and he didn't have a car for them to perform in, but as Yahoo had said - if he doesn't make the effort then nothing will ever come of it anyway. It was an extreme idea, but he was developing a talent for ideas. A backup plan was essential and he'd come up with it. This video was going to get made, one way or another and sooner rather than later.

When his shift was over, he was already exhausted and not by his day at work. The last week had been an emotional roller coaster ride of the highest highs and the lowest lows that he'd ever experienced in his life. Trying not to get excited about the next part of his mission in case it failed, he limped home from work with a 'what will be will be' attitude in the hope that it would stop him going mad. He even managed to ignore the incessant mooing of Two Bums who'd crossed the road to join him and followed him all the way to the flat.

Thankfully, Yahoo had gone back to what he knew best and had meatballs with pasta shells awaiting on the table.

"I thought it would make a change from spaghetti," he said, as Cas took his seat.

Cas nodded. "I always wondered why they had so many different shapes. I suppose it's like us with potatoes and all the different things we do with them to make them not boring."

"Really! Are there lots of things you can do with potatoes?"

"Have you never cooked a potato?" Cas asked, unsure if Yahoo was serious or taking the mickey, as he so often did.

"I've peeled them to make gnocchi, but apart from that, I wouldn't know what to do with them."

"You really are a strange one. Have you never made chips, jacket potatoes, roasties or even mash?"

"No. I wouldn't have a clue how to and what would I serve it with anyway. Pass the Parmesan, please."

Cas passed him the cheese shaker and realised how heartbroken Yahoo must have been when he'd heard the Italian girl had left and got married. His life wasn't a constant high of good fortune; he'd had bad luck and knew what disappointment felt like. To think he'd gone through years of sweating in a restaurant kitchen when he had no interest in food whatsoever, and all for nothing, made him a little more human in Cas's eyes. He changed the subject away from food and tucked into his meatballs.

"How was your luck today then?"

"I have a feeling that my luck is running late today. It's

around though. I had a lie-in this morning and I went to see Lexy at lunchtime. I was dying to know what the area manager had to say. I had a nose around before she had any customers. That place has a great kitchen, you know. I can't understand why the Landlord didn't make the most of it. I'd go there every Sunday for a proper roast dinner. He could have made a bomb selling food."

"Well, what did they say to her?"

"You'll never guess what! She went for it. She explained what had happened and that she thought it best to keep the place running until she could get hold of someone, and then she asked them straight if there was a way she could take on the lease. Apparently, they were a bit taken aback at first, but she explained what the guy was like and that she'd been running it for months on her own anyway. They've arranged a proper meeting with her on Wednesday. I think she was in shock. I know she's amazed that they'd taken her seriously, but—why not? Lexy is the best person to be there and it doesn't sound like they have anyone waiting to take a pub on. I honestly believe that girl can really make something of that place and I think it'll do her the world of good. She might stop being so cheeky to the customers when it's her profit she's thinking about. You can't go around calling your punters pigs."

"I don't want her to change. You know she didn't mean it."

"I know that, but some people might not be so thick-skinned as me. And there are a lot of potential customers out there. I checked on the catchment area on the internet and with so many pubs closed down around here, she's got a huge market. If she needed some investment into the place to improve it, I'm sure we could come up with some kind of deal."

Cas had the feeling that Yahoo was more interested with the figures of money that the pub could generate and less about Lexy's welfare. It was the way Yahoo was, but he didn't like it. He wanted to go and hear her good news for himself, but his own needs would have to come first. Once he'd eaten his dinner, he thanked Yahoo and put his plate in the dishwasher.

"Is it okay to take the scooter out? There's something I need to get." He wasn't lying.

"Sure, but be really careful. She's booked into the garage for Thursday and for a respray on Friday. I don't want an even bigger bill on my hands."

"Neither do I," Cas said catching the key.

He checked his map before leaving and hung his phone around his neck. Prepared and determined, he collected the scooter and headed out of town on the road that led to the reservoir; He rode with great care and patience.

It took a while, but soon he spotted the sign for the car park that Lexy had told him to avoid. He turned onto the small lane and drove through the trees where a stretch of gravel indicated a place to park. There were several cars lined up, but none of them had occupants. He parked his scooter up and strapped his helmet to it. Not wanting to be hanging about looking conspicuous, he went for a hobble down to the reservoir in the attempt to look like an innocent rambler. Keeping the car park in view, with the hope that the silver Mini Coupe would turn up, he wandered painfully along the track by the water's edge, passing many cyclists and dog walkers. It really wasn't what he'd expected to find there.

It occurred to him that there must be a particular time for the doggers to arrive. He'd imagined the place to be a secluded area where no one else came and couples dogged at all times of the day and night, but this place was nothing like that. It was busy with people that you'd expect to be at a reservoir nature reserve. He was happy to wander until nightfall if his ankle could take it, but he couldn't hang around until two in the morning, as he had to get up for work the next day.

Jumping over a stile without thinking, he screamed out in pain as his ankle gave way and sent shooting pains up his leg and into his back. That brought an end to his ramble. He hopped to a grassy bank and sat down to rest his joint while he watched the people loading their cars with dogs and bicycles and leaving the car park empty. The sun set behind a hill and everything was still and silent, as the sky became dark.

Feeling the chill of the night enter his body, he got up and struggled to make his way back and to warm himself up. To his delight ahead of him, two, then four, then six headlight beams appeared close by where he'd parked the scooter. He squinted his eyes and strained to make out the colour and model of the cars in the darkness. It was impossible to differentiate anything other than light car or dark car. Quickening his step by skipping, he made it back up to the outskirts of the car park.

Switching the camera on to be more than prepared he limped, as naturally as he could, back to the scooter where he viewed the scene in front of him while sneakily making out he was checking his tyres, so as not to look suspicious. None of the occupants had left their vehicles and the inside lights were switched on one by one. He was sure that the middle car was a Mini Coupe, but even this close he couldn't tell the colour. It vexed him that it was jammed between the other two cars and hadn't parked on the outside making his job easier. This was what he'd been waiting for. So close to mission complete, he had to chance getting between the cars without being caught.

Reminding himself that these people really came here to be viewed 'doing it' and would take no offence at him being there watching, he crept up to the cars. Pointing his mobile towards the middle car, he got closer. Close enough to get the full back window on his screen. It was hard to tell what was happening on the mobile screen, but he wasn't interested in watching them; he wanted to get the perfect shot. Holding it firmly and concentrating on keeping the angle, he expected he'd have to hold the stance for a while.

He was focusing so hard on his screen that he was unaware that one of the other car doors had opened. A fierce voice broke the silence.

"What the fuck do you think you're doing, you pervert?"

Looking around, Cas's eyes weren't adjusted to the darkness, but from the dashboard light of the next car, he saw the open door and a very big man was struggling on all fours across the seat trying to pull his trousers up and exit the car. He could see by the man's angry face that he wasn't asking for an explanation really. Turning, hobbling, hopping and skipping, Cas got to the scooter before the man got to him. Jumping on, he revved her up and sped off, not even attempting to put his helmet on. The Vespa spun and skidded on the gravel, as he fought with it to take control. Not being able to tell which direction he was heading, miraculously the scooter hit tarmac and he found himself on the small lane that he'd originally driven up. He hit the corner to the main road without braking and luckily the road was clear of traffic. Forgetting all his promises to Yahoo, he pushed the little scooter to her limits.

Seeing the lights of the town ahead of him, he relaxed slightly. Fortune had been on his side at last and got him out of something that could have resulted in a very nasty situation. The footage he'd taken hadn't been that long, but the way his luck was going, it would be enough. All he had to do was to get back to the flat safely and his whole future would be changed and the BEET office would be a thing of the past.

Moments before reaching the safety of the town, he saw in the wing mirror a set of headlights not far behind him, then another and another and they were gaining on him fast.

Hitting the streets before they were on top of him, he tried weaving through the back roads in the hope that he'd lose them. His cornering and balancing skills had improved remarkably which could have been down to experience, but even he realised it was more likely a survival instinct burst of adrenalin that kept him from leaving the road.

He was so close to home and she just needed to give him a little more. Pushing his luck and the Vespa for one more corner, he could see the garage in sight. He fumbled in his pocket for the fob and veered into a lamppost. Her engine cut out completely, as Cas flew through the air and landed in the road. The three cars pulled up around him.

The men got out of the cars and swaggered towards him. Cas opened his mouth to explain, but it was filled with a fist. Rolling over across the road, he was kicked like a football from one boot to the other while the men laughed and jeered and shouted names at him.

As his head spun over and his face scraped against the tarmac, he spotted Yahoo standing on the pavement.

"Yahoo! Yahoo!" he yelled out, not believing his luck, but Yahoo walked away from him very slowly.

"Yahoo! Yahoo!"

He was given another kick in the leg.

"Yahoo!" he cried out at the top of his voice.

The men kicked him even more and began shouting

themselves.

"Wahey! Yahoo! Whoopee! Wahey!"

"Yahoo! Please, Yahoo!" Cas tried to see where his friend had gone, but there was no sign of him.

Two of the women got out of the cars and joined in the beating hollering, "Yahoo, Wahey, Yipee."

Cas screamed out louder, "Yahoo, Yahoo, Yahoo!"

The street seemed to get brighter and as Cas stared up between the stars in the sky and the houses and flats on either side, he saw it was because every light was on with people's heads looking out of their windows at the commotion below.

The kicking ceased.

"You're some kind of nutcase, Boy. Give me that phone," the man standing above him said, before wrenching it so hard that Cas thought he'd be strangled to death. The cord snapped and he gasped for breath.

"Yahoo!" he sobbed.

The man placed the mobile right up close to Cas's face and stamped on it several times until it was well and truly smashed to pieces.

Cas started to cry and had one more attempt at getting help. "Yaaaaaahoooo!"

As the neighbours watched on in horror, his five attackers walked back to their cars, shaking their heads and drove away.

Pulling himself up out of the road, he crawled to the pavement beside the crashed Vespa. He brushed himself down and stared at the crumpled front of his so-called mate's scooter. Yahoo appeared from the darkness.

"Are you okay, Mate?"

"I'm alive. No thanks to you. Why didn't you help me?"

"What? And both of us end up with a kick-in. I wouldn't have been any help against those guys. Anyhow, don't worry about it. I think we might have just got you famous. I'll show you tomorrow. Now give me the garage key and get yourself home—you've got work in the morning. I'll put this baby away. She ain't dead yet."

"Me neither, but I don't feel far from it."

"You'll be fine, Mate. If they'd wanted to kill you, they would have." Yahoo pushed the scooter towards the garage and Cas tentatively made his way to the steps of the flat where he was greeted with a 'Moo' from Two Bums. He slammed the door behind him and went straight to bed.

Down

Although the BEET office was like prison, or maybe an asylum is a better description, Cas relaxed in the knowledge that he was safely inside with an airlock between him and the outside world. With a bruising eye, a fat lip, a sore ankle and every muscle in his body aching, he sat at his desk cocooned in his headset and comfy chair. He didn't care that the day was boring, that the job was pointless and unsatisfying, as it gave him the chance to rest. There wasn't the frustration that he was missing out on anything because his phone was smashed to pieces and it would be a while before he could afford to get a new one.

He was only disturbed once by Wendy. Making him jump out of his solitude, she squeezed at his shoulder with her red claws.

"You look terrible. Have you been in an accident?"

Cas shook his head. His jaw was so painful and he wasn't in the mood to talk.

Wendy continued in her sexy voice. "I was hoping to see you at the karaoke tonight. It's your turn to sing."

Trying to smile, Cas muttered, "It hurts."

She squeezed his shoulder harder which also hurt. "I'll think of something to cheer you up. I'm going out for a cigarette. Do you want some fresh air?"

"No. I'm okay." Cas sensed her predatory nature. She

had her claws into him and he was weak and vulnerable, but she left it at that, wiggled off and disappeared through the airlock.

He gave up on answering the phone. Each time a call came in, he made a squeaking noise and hung up hoping it sounded like a technical problem.

Resigned to the fact that he was never going to get the video that he desired, he pondered on his future at the BEET office. Surely, if he tried harder, one day he might be promoted to trainer or maybe a team leader, but he realised it was a ridiculous idea. He was never going to be taught anything more than the little he already had been. A body at a desk was his job description and even such a simple task was painful that day. The other option was to look for another job. Now that he had one, he had more chance of finding another one. That's what he'd heard anyway. He forced himself to believe that since coming to Berrycroft, his life was on the up. He adjusted the headset many times, as it was putting pressure on the bump on his head, and got through the hours neither high nor low. It was a kind of limbo void of emotion, but full of physical pain each time he moved.

His day over, he entered the airlock and an enormous guy with the widest arse Cas had ever seen squeezed his way in behind him.

"You're the new lad, right? I'm Sam. How'd you like it so far?"

Out of politeness, he bore the pain to answer.

"It's okay, but I'm looking for something else. It'll do for the time being."

The man boomed out a laugh.

"That's exactly what I said when I first started here. Twenty-two years later and look at me—still here."

Smiling in agreement, rather than seeing the funny

side, Cas limped out of the airlock and made his way home. Twenty-two years echoed around his brain with the image of that arse getting bigger and wider with each year.

Recalling what Yahoo had said the night before, he shook the thoughts from his brain and entered the flat with a flicker of excitement in the hope that his friend had come up with a plan to make him famous.

Predictably, Yahoo was in his apron in the kitchen.

"I didn't think you'd wanna chew, so I've make you minestrone soup and soft bread. You got quite a kick-in last night. Who were those guys? I recognised one, but I can't—for the life of me think where from."

"I don't have a clue. There was a misunderstanding. I was videoing something and they got the wrong idea. It's hard to talk."

Taking a sweet tin down from the shelf, Yahoo searched through packets, sachets and plasters then handed Cas a strip of pills.

"Take a couple of those. They'll kill the pain in no time and help with the swelling."

Cas swallowed them down with the soup.

"Thanks. It wouldn't have been so bad if you'd helped me, instead of just walking off."

"I didn't just walk off. You'll see in a moment. If I'd got involved, I'd be looking and feeling as shit as you now. And I have my reputation to think of—imagine what the neighbours would say."

"I don't need to imagine. I know what they think of me."

Wiping the last of his bread around the bowl, Cas watched as Yahoo still licked his own bowl even though he'd mopped up all the soup.

"Come—this might make the pain go away. It could have all been worth it after all," Yahoo said, as he led the way to his office with a big grin on his face.

"Don't tell me you filmed me getting beaten up."

"Better than that, Cas. I have made you your very own debut video. Watch this."

As Cas watched the video, he was flummoxed at how different it was from the actual event he remembered. A jolly country and western song played in the background and the guy on the floor being beaten did look like he was being injured severely, but also seemed to be enjoying the thrashing, crying out 'Yahoo' with each kick. The three attackers joined in the chanting with 'Wahey' and 'Yeeha' and although it was painful for him to watch, Cas couldn't stop himself from seeing the funny side and laughing.

It was over much quicker than he expected. His experience the night before had seemed to go on for ten times as long. It finished with a close up of Cas's distressed and bloody face mouthing the word 'Yahoo'.

"You've made something hilarious out of something very painful and horrid, but what are you going to do with it? Please don't put it on the internet. I'll end up a laughing stock."

"I'm not going to put it on the internet. You are! Remember how I told you I started out—riding a bar stool and yelling 'Yahoo'. Well, this is where you're gonna start. We'll call you Wahey or Yipee or Yeeha—it's your choice, but you can't have Yahoo. You post the video under that name. I'll band it around my subscribers and it'll spread without you having to do a thing. After that, it is down to you to find or make your own videos. I'll help you and teach you how all this kit works. You're on your way out of that office, Cas. What do you think?"

Not wanting to be ungrateful, but very aware of why he got beaten up in the first place, Cas tried to slow down the situation and Yahoo's eagerness.

"It's really kind of you to have done this for me and it's a cracking video that must have taken you some time edit, but I don't have anything else yet. It would be daft if I put that one out there and I don't get anything decent for a year or two. I think I'll save it until the time's right. I am really grateful and you say it's mine, right?"

"It's all yours. It's a present from me."

"So, you won't post it? That's down to me—when I'm ready to use it?"

"Yes. It's yours okay and I won't post it, alright. I'll not touch it, watch it or think about again, but I thought you'd jump at the chance to upload it."

"No point in being hasty. I'm not as lucky as you and it might take me a while to build up a portfolio of videos. If I'm gonna get any success out of this, I need to be prepared and learn the tricks. You forget I haven't found my sense yet. When I do, I'll go for it."

What was actually running through Cas's mind was his mother watching this funny but violent video of her son and the chance that the three guys might also get wind of it and leave a comment stating that they'd beaten him up because he was sneakily filming people doing things of a sexual nature. He was sure she'd disown him or even have a heart attack. He couldn't risk it.

Yahoo walked out of the office.

"I can see where you're coming from and it was me that told you to be prepared, so I can't knock you for being more cautious than I'd be. You aren't the luckiest guy I've ever met—quite the contrary. I can't blame you for taking a step back—look at the state of you. That eye will be a right shiner by tomorrow. I bet your own mother wouldn't recognise you now."

Cas followed. "Hopefully, I'll be looking normal again by the weekend. It's her birthday on Sunday and I was hoping to surprise her by turning up sometime. I'll try and keep out of harm's way until then. There's not much I can do until I get a new phone anyway."

"Well, if you do feel a sense, I have cameras you can borrow and they're insured if that makes you feel any better."

"Thanks, but I'm not attempting anything for the rest of the week. I'm not showing up on her birthday in a wheelchair and the way my luck's running that'll be the next stage."

"Cas, you have to stop being so negative and down on yourself. You'll repel good luck, otherwise. Why do you think it's called negative and positive? It works like a magnet and you need to switch the poles."

"You sound very impressive Yahoo, but you're talking shit. When I was at my most positive, I ended up in this state. How's that prove your theory?"

"You were still lucky. Every scrape you've found yourself in could have turned out a hell of a lot worse if you were in a negative mood. I think you've been really lucky. Your eyebrows will grow back and the bruises will disappear. It's only surface damage."

"You have some strange ways of looking at things. I'm going for a shower," Cas said, walking to his room.

"Are you coming down the pub? It's Karaoke night—might be a bit of a laugh. It might cheer you up a bit."

"Definitely not. Who knows what Bendy Wendy has in store for me or what other mishap will come my way the minute I leave the flat? I'll have a shower, get into bed, watch a film and have an early night. It'll give my body time to heal and hopefully, Miss Fortune will go and find someone else to play with."

"If that's what you think's best, then I'll see you tomorrow sometime. Have a great day at the BEET office and bring some eggs home for me. Bye!"

"Grrr…" Closing his bedroom door, Cas spent the evening feeling sorry for himself, but safe.

Enough

Sitting at his desk, Cas's pain was slightly less after a good night's kip though he looked a lot worse. The skin around his left eye was a vivid lilac with a yellow halo and his right had turned completely black. Apart from the odd look he got from the security guard on the way in, no one in the office seemed to notice or care what had happened to him. Trying to concentrate on his screen and get the day over with, he couldn't help himself from glancing over to where Sam was sat and the huge arse that was spilling over the edge of his chair. Though Cas had only been at the office a week and a half, it already seemed like years. He could only image what twenty-two years in that place could do to a man's soul. Haunting images of bears behind bars rocking back and forth, pacing up and down filled his head. Watching Sam constantly eat crisps, biscuits, chocolate bars and cakes throughout the morning, when there was no way he could possibly be hungry, depressed him. In twenty-two years time he would be Sam.

His moods swung throughout the day. He was down, angry, suffocating, claustrophobic, hopeless, all negative. He remembered what Lexy had said about the place driving you insane and only a mad person would last more than a week. He'd taken it as part of her cynical nature, but she was spot-on. He was going mad and didn't think his day could get any worse.

Wendy's hand gripped his shoulder.

"I missed you last night."

"Sorry. I needed an early one. I wasn't feeling too well at all."

"Tell me about it. You don't look too well. Have you been in an accident?"

"Yes! I had a crash and then I got attacked, beaten and mugged of my mobile. Hopefully, that's enough and nothing worse can happen." He wasn't lying really.

"You poor thing, but hiding away isn't the answer. You need to get out and enjoy yourself, especially, working in this place. You'll go mental otherwise. You are foolish for not coming out last night. You'd be so much happier today if you had. You missed the best karaoke ever. The Krankies turned up and they were such a scream. They're even funnier in real life than on the telly. They sang some hilarious songs—changing all the words to make them naughty. They're such a lovely couple. It would have cheered you up no end."

Huffing down his nostrils, it was the last straw. Pulling off his headset, his face dropped into his hands and he let out a loud groan.

Wendy squeezed his injured shoulder harder.

"What's wrong? You aren't going to puke, are you?"

"Yes! I might. I feel terrible."

"Well, I suggest you go home. Things spread around fast in this environment. I don't want the whole team going down with it." She had already stepped away from him.

"That's a very good idea, Wendy. Are you sure you don't mind?" He got up, turned off his workstation and began to drag his body away from it.

"I'm positive. I'm sure this lot will manage without you. Make sure you use the disinfectant before you swipe your hand out."

Not bothered by the fact that Wendy thought he had a disease, rather than physical and mental pain, he calculated that he would lose less than thirty quid, cleaned and swiped his hand, and got out of the place as fast as his sore ankle would carry him without causing him to yell out in pain.

Outside the building, he stood and rested. He breathed in the fresh air and thought how there must be an easier way of earning thirty quid in an afternoon.

The ground beneath him began to vibrate and he watched as a hole appeared in the road, spreading wider and deeper. A disused factory across the street disappeared down into it with an almighty roar and then everything fell silent. He found himself standing on the edge of a crater in total astonishment before a water-main split and sent up a spout that hit him and knocked him on his arse.

Crawling away, someone pulled him to his feet.

"I guess I better let you have this footage too. You're becoming quite a star, Cas," Yahoo said.

"I would have got that if I'd had my mobile," Cas replied.

"It shows you're getting better. You were almost in the right place—just not prepared. You'll get it right one day. It could have been worse—you could have been crossing the road. Anyway, why aren't you in work? Did you get the sack?"

"No. They think I'm diseased, so they told me to go home. They didn't think I'd be missed. I'll probably go in tomorrow and find Jimmy Krankie sitting at my workstation."

"It's funny you say that. They turned up at the karaoke last night. They're a right pair. It was one of the best nights ever."

"I've heard!"

"Let's get you home and dry you off—you look a mess." Yahoo put his arm around him and took the weight off his ankle.

Back at the flat, Cas showered and changed before going through to the kitchen and putting the kettle on. Yahoo joined him.

"Do you want to see what I shot? It's great—it's like 'Oh my God' and then when it seems to be all over, that jet of water appears and knocks you for six. The timing's perfect on its own. I hardly need to edit it."

"I'd rather not be reminded. I think I've cracked my coccyx. I won't be able to sit at my desk at all tomorrow."

"You can't go in tomorrow if you have a disease anyway. What is it?"

"Nothing. I don't have anything germy-related. That place is just driving me insane. I can't give it up, though—I owe too much money, but I am going to look for something else."

"Well, Bob should be out soon enough. I thought he was going to sort you something out at the post office," Yahoo said with a cheeky smirk on his face.

"Not funny!"

"Oh, come on—it can't be that bad. Leave the coffee. I was going to pop down The White Horse, if it's open, see how Lexy got on with the brewery guy. Are you coming or are you gonna spend the rest of the day feeling sorry for yourself?"

"Okay. I could do with a proper drink and I wouldn't want to miss out on anything else."

Yahoo went to his office and came back with a camera. He handed it to Cas with a wink, as they left the flat.

"The door's open. It's looking good," Yahoo said, as they crossed the street to The White Horse.

Inside, Lexy was in a daze and biting her nails.

"Two beers, please. Chop, chop, girl! What's got into you?"

"That could be a bit of a problem. I can't serve you any alcohol. I don't have a license."

For the first time ever, Cas truly wanted a beer and he was being denied it. Without saying a word, he looked at her with resignation and disappointment, and then turned to Yahoo.

Not being the type to give in that easily, Yahoo stood his ground.

"What's the point of being open then?"

"It's only temporary—so people don't spread the word that the pub has closed down. You can have a coke."

Reaching into his pocket, Yahoo pulled out a handful of change and spread it on the bar. There must have been over ten quid.

"Would you sell me two beer mats then, please? You choose your price. And remember, every beer mat comes with a free pint."

Lexy deciphered what he'd said.

"Can I really do that?"

"I can't see why not. You only need a license to sell alcohol. You don't need one to give it away."

"You are so damn clever. Why didn't I think of that?" she said, as she started pouring the drinks.

Yahoo smiled. Cas thought the same thing, 'Why hadn't I been clever enough to think of that?'

She sorted through the change and took the price of two beers.

Holding up the beer mat, Yahoo shook his head.

"That is an awfully expensive piece of cardboard.

Anyhow, how did it go with the area manager? You're still here and still open—just. I take it it's good news?"

"It's not that simple, but it's better than I expected. Firstly, I have to have a license. It's only a daylong course and I'm booked in for Friday, so I'll have to close in the daytime. I've got the book to revise from, but it is so complicated—it's more about the law than the running of a pub. If I don't pass, then that's the end of it."

"You will pass. Reason being—you'll learn it cos you want it. Also, those kind of courses are run so you do pass. If you have a problem, just call the guy over and ask him to refresh your memory. He'll tell you the answer. He has to keep his own success rate high to keep his job. It'll be nothing like the exams you had at school."

Hearing this, Lexy's face lit up and dropped almost as quickly.

"Then there's the money. I have to pay them a deposit for two months' rent and the price of the lease. I've rang every bank to arrange a meeting for a loan and I didn't even get an appointment. Every one of them said they don't lend money for pubs regardless of the situation. I'm going to go online later and see if I can find a finance company that'll lend me it."

Yahoo whistled an almost silent breath of air through his teeth.

"You really don't want to do that. You'll never make any money paying back their ridiculous interest rates. How much are they after all together?"

"Well, it's about four grand for the rent deposit and ten thousand for the lease. I'll need another thousand for fees and stuff."

"That sounds like an awfully cheap lease. How come?"

"It's not the lease as such. It's for fixtures and fittings. The Landlord hadn't paid his rent for six months, so he's violated the terms of his lease. I'm not buying it from him—like you normally would. I'm not buying his business. The area manager said he can give me a new lease. They can just give me it virtually free, but I have to pay for the fixtures and fittings."

"I'll lend you fifteen grand interest-free if you do one thing for me."

Both Lexy and Cas stood open-mouthed waiting for what he was to demand.

"You employ a chef on Sundays to make roast dinners—someone who knows what they're doing and I want a free roast dinner every week. Apart from that, I don't want to interfere in the business at all."

Yahoo held out his hand and Lexy snatched at it. "Deal," she said, without batting an eyelid.

"Great. So you should be open as normal on Saturday."

"I still have to pass the licence exam and send it to the council for approval, but they said that would go through fine, as long as I didn't hide any criminal record I have and I haven't got one. Once I have the certificate, I can sell beer."

"You will pass the exam. I'll transfer the money into your account this evening if you write down your details."

"Okay. Oh, hang on. There was one more thing. They don't like to take on sole individuals. They asked me about my partner and I wasn't sure if they meant business-wise or relationship-wise. Obviously, I wasn't going to mention that fool of a boyfriend. I haven't even seen him for over a week anyhow and I can't say I'm that bothered."

Cas gazed at Yahoo. He could see what was happening. The guy hadn't even tried and yet he was about to become a partner in a pub. How he managed to be in the right place all of the time totally amazed him.

Lexy continued.

"So, I gave them your name, Cas. I hope you don't mind. I didn't state what kind of partnership we were, but ... well, you just popped into my head."

"What!" Had Cas heard that right? He shook his head.

"I'm sorry and don't panic—it's only for their records. You don't have to have anything to do with the place."

Yahoo punched him on the arm and out of his stupor.

"This is just what you need. It's perfect. Can't you see that, you fool?"

"Wait a minute. I haven't quite got what she's getting me involved in. Don't you start!"

"It's exactly what the place needs. She can't run it entirely on her own."

Yahoo turned to Lexy. "I know you have been running it on your own, but it's no life having to be here day and night with no one to turn to if there's a problem or you're ill. You really do need a partner."

Lexy nodded. "It would be so much easier. I could have much more going on here if I didn't have to do everything myself."

Holding up his hands and looking very pale, Cas tried to stop them getting carried away with his life.

"I know nothing about working in a pub, let alone running one. I've never even poured a pint."

Taking hold of both his hands, Yahoo placed them on the bar.

"I'm sure Lexy didn't either before she started working here. Stop fretting and think where you'd rather be—BEET office or here?"

"Well, obviously anywhere has to be better than the BEET office."

"Exactly! Look, I've got money wrapped up in this place that I'd like to have back as soon as possible and you need a job. A satisfying job. A job that you make something out of what you put in. You can cook Sunday roasts. That's your first job. I've seen that kitchen—it's pucker and only the fryer looks like it's ever been used. I'll teach you how to make the best authentic pizzas tomorrow—not like the naff ones they sell around here. Real pizzas with my special recipe dough and tomato sauce. During the week, you will sell pizzas. On Sundays, you make the best roasts in town. You can even start a pizza delivery service if you want. You'll be working for yourself and I know it's going to be a success for all of us. I can sense it."

"Whoa! You're really racing ahead there, Yahoo. You want me to be a Landlord, a pizza chef and start up a delivery service? Are you nuts?"

"Why not? Who's telling you that you can't - except yourself?"

The three of them looked back and forth between each other's glances for a few seconds before they all burst out laughing, high-fived each other and hugged. Yahoo was the only one who wasn't shaking.

Lexy opened a dusty bottle of champagne and poured it all into three tumblers.

"To us!" she squealed and the guys repeated it.

Cas had never been so terrified in his whole life.

Necking down their toast, Cas screwed up his face. Never tasting it before, he wasn't sure if the champagne was bad or was meant to be so sour. The others confirmed it was bad. Lexy spat the last mouthful into a slop bucket and Yahoo swallowed down his pronouncing, "That was kack. I'll get something decent in for Saturday night."

"I'm glad you thought that. I wasn't sure what it was meant to taste like." Cas admitted.

"You'll be tasting a lot more of it when you're rich, Cas. Now there's no point sitting around here while there's work to be done. I suggest you and me get to cleaning that kitchen up and leave Lexy to deal with the bar."

Following Yahoo through the bar to the kitchen, Cas had a horrible uneasy sense of trespassing reminding him of when he went to a pantomime with his mother as a boy. He'd gone looking for the toilets and found himself somewhere that he shouldn't have been and was screamed at by Captain Hook. He refused from that day on to go to anything at the theatre again. Like a small boy, he stood in the kitchen and looked around it nervously. Yahoo was totally unfazed by being there and started organising the place.

"Cas, get rid of that fryer somewhere while I clean the fridge. I'll buy a new one tomorrow and we'll have this fridge stocked up to. You can forget all about getting up and going into that office in the morning. I'll teach you the art of pizza making here and we'll give them away free. It'll be a great promotion to start you off."

"Hold on! Aren't we getting a little ahead of ourselves? I have to go to work tomorrow. Lexy might not pass the exam. Anything could happen and I can't lose my job."

"So full of doubt all the time, aren't you? That's why you scare away luck. This is your job now. Get the BEET office out of your brain. Here! Call them and tell them you've quit." Yahoo held out his mobile.

"I can't do that."

"You can do anything you want. You're a man, aren't you?"

Cas took the mobile and tapped in the numbers. Something inside him was telling him not to do it. At the same time, everything around him was telling him to do it.

"Hello. It's Cas Howard. I won't be in tomorrow. I'm going to the doctor's."

He hung up. "Just keeping my options open. I know my luck."

After hours of cleaning, they returned to the bar area.

"Have you got a spare key for the place?" Yahoo asked Lexy.

She reached up and took a box down from a shelf.

"The Landlord's bunch," she said, holding them up and then handing them to Cas.

Looking down at the keys in his hand, Cas struggled to grasp that what was going on was real. Yahoo nudged his elbow.

"Shall we go home and have some dinner? We've got a lot to do in the morning and I don't want you having one of your hangovers from hell."

Putting the keys in his pocket, Cas nodded.

"Sure. I'll have an early night."

Turning to Lexy, Yahoo held his arm out for another handshake.

"We'll be in sometime in the morning with supplies. We'll be giving away free pizzas all day if you want to advertise the fact. What a deal—free beer and pizza for the price of a beer mat."

"That's a great idea. Thank you, guys. Do you need the Cash and Carry card too?"

"Nice one. That'll save a lot of running around. See you tomorrow," Yahoo said, taking the card.

"Bye." Lexy gave them a twiddling finger wave.

"Good night," said Cas, again strangely uneasy that he was walking out of a pub with the keys to the front door in his pocket.

Lesson

When Cas woke to the smell of strong coffee, he found Yahoo sitting at the kitchen table and writing a list of everything they needed to collect. Looking over his shoulder, Cas struggled to read or recognise half of the things that he'd written and couldn't believe that they'd need so much stuff for making pizza.

"You're up and at it early," Cas remarked.

"No! You're up late. I've already seen to the guy who was picking up the scooter, edited a video and ordered a freezer for the kitchen. You'll have to get yourself more prepared if you're going to run a business."

"Don't kid me. You're never up before I go to work normally."

"Normally, no I'm not, but I still have things to do other than ferry you around the shops and teach you the art of pizza making. You'll learn that in order to relax sometimes, you'll have to get organised else you'll be forever running around trying to catch up. It's your first day, though, and I have confidence in you."

"Well, thank you. I'm glad you do. I would have been up earlier if I'd realised you'd be waiting around for me."

"No problem. We have plenty of time. You need to write a list of what you need for Sunday dinner, and I mean everything including whatever you cook it in, utensils and what you'll serve it on. Plates I guess, but you need to think of everything. You need to get it perfect. If you realise you only have spoons for them to eat with, as you serve up the dinners, you won't have time to do anything about it and your customers won't come back."

"I getcha. This is going to cost a fortune, though, and we're still not a hundred percent sure that Lexy will be given the go-ahead," Cas said sitting down to write his list.

"You'll pay me back soon enough—if you get it right. I have faith that Lexy won't let us down. Forget what might go wrong. It might not."

Writing out his list, Cas tried to fight off the bad thoughts that told him he was bound to forget something. He put the pen in his pocket, so he could add anything that might have slipped his mind on the way.

As they left the flat, Yahoo turned to him. "Have you got the camera I gave you?"

"Yes. It's in my pocket."

"Good! You see, you're learning fast."

On the way to the Cash and Carry, Cas read through his list and imagined he was in his mother's kitchen, but on a grander scale. Although he was sure he had everything that he needed, he still had that niggle of self-doubt that he'd forgotten something.

Yahoo stopped the car in the middle of nowhere and got out. Cas watched him jump out in a hurry and walk through the hedgerow. He guessed he must have been desperate for a pee, so he turned away.

Returning to the car, Yahoo handed Cas his phone.

"Take a look at that little beauty."

"What the ..." Cas spun his head around and eyed the bushes, but there was nothing there.

Grinning, Yahoo started up the car. "Black panther. It walked straight past me."

"Well done, Mate." Cas handed the phone back.

Nothing surprised him anymore when it came to Yahoo and his super-sense.

After they'd got the majority of the supplies from the Cash and Carry, they went to the Italian wholesaler for Yahoo's special ingredients. He explained what they were to Cas and told him how to pronounce them properly. With the boot and the backseat fully loaded, they made their way to The White Horse.

"When will you be moving out?" Yahoo asked to Cas's astonishment.

"Moving out? I wasn't planning on moving out."

"The flat above the pub must be bigger than mine. Why pay me rent when you can live there? The rent you pay for the pub covers the flat too. You'd be mad not to use it."

"I see what you mean, but I'd have to speak to Lexy about it. She'll probably be moving in herself."

"It'll be plenty big enough for both of you and you are Landlord and Landlady, after all. You should both live there."

"Nothing's official yet. You are jumping the gun a lot."

"Better that than get left behind. When she passes that exam tomorrow, it's as good as official. We'll have an 'Under new management' party Saturday night. Then, it's all down to you two."

"I guess I'll move in on Saturday then if she agrees to it. It's all happening so fast and my head can't keep up."

"You'll be fine once you get busy."

"I haven't even been here two weeks. It's quite mental."

"Sometimes you find yourself in the right place at the right time. That's life."

They drove the rest of the way in silence, as Cas recollected his thoughts over the past fortnight. He chuckled to himself, as he recalled how many times he'd wished he was in the right place at the right time, thinking all along that he never was and Yahoo had all the luck. The reality of it was that he was exactly where he should have been. He just couldn't see it at the time.

Pulling up outside the pub, Yahoo smiled a broad grin. "Let us in then, Landlord."

Cas shook his head, got out of the car and unlocked the door of The White Horse. A bizarre sense of wrongness made him nervous, but at the same time excited.

They unloaded the supplies.

"I'll leave you to sort out where you want to store stuff. I'm taking the car home and I need to get this panther to the newspaper. I'll be back before opening and we'll make pizza. I'll add all this lot to your bill." Yahoo laughed and left.

As Cas filled the fridge and stacked the shelves, it started to sink in that this was real. A strange sadness crept over him. Not that he was sad about it, but more that he was overwhelmed by all the help he'd been given from a guy he didn't even know a fortnight ago.

"Cooey."

He jumped, dropping the handful of pizza pans he was holding. They clattered and rolled around the floor. It was Lexy.

"I hope that doesn't happen when they've got pizzas in them." She laughed.

"No. You scared the life out of me. I was in my own little world."

"I thought I'd come in and give the place a good clean. We can get a cleaner when we're up and running. He sacked the last one cos he couldn't see the point, but you'd never get in the gents now if it weren't for me doing it."

Cas found it remarkable how Lexy had said 'we're' and it all became a little bit realer.

"Yahoo suggested that I move in here. Well, that I should, as I'm going to be kind of the Landlord. I said I'd check with you in case you were moving in."

"There's plenty of room for both of us. Why wouldn't you move in? And don't say kind of the Landlord. You are the Landlord or you will be officially once all the paperwork is out of the way. That's just formalities, though. You've done a great job in here. I didn't realise how grubby the kitchen was until you guys cleaned it. I could eat off the floor. What's that noise?"

"I can't hear anything."

She opened the back door and Cas heard a very familiar sound.

"Moo!"

"Oh, Cas look! We have our first customer. The poor thing looks starving. Have you got anything I can give him?"

"He's a she. That's the stray Bob feeds. She can starve, for all I care. Horrid animal."

"How can you be so cruel? It's not her fault she's not cute and mews like a cow. I'll find her something. It'll be good to have a cat around. It'll keep the rats and mice away."

"You can feed her, but don't let her in. She's probably riddled with fleas and diseases."

Lexy took some meat out to her. "What's your name then?"

Leaning against the back door, ready to slam it shut if the creature attempted to come any closer, Cas replied for the cat.

"It's Jess. As in Postman Pat and his black and white cow. If you type it into the internet, you'll see she's quite famous." He couldn't bear to tell the story of her real name.

"Really? How cool! She's quite hungry—poor little thing. I'm sure we'll have plenty of leftovers we can throw her way every day, at least until Bob gets home."

Cas didn't answer. When she came back in and went back to cleaning the bar, he made sure the cat didn't follow and shut and locked the door.

Continuing sorting his kitchen to the hum of the vacuum cleaner in the distance, he thought about his crazy notion to catch The Krankies dogging. He wouldn't have the chance to pursue his dream video now, but it didn't seem quite so important anymore.

Hearing knocking, he went through to the bar and saw the frosted silhouette of Yahoo at the window. He let him in and his training began.

Yahoo was a fantastic and patient teacher. 'Be prepared' was his outlook with everything. They spent a huge amount of time making a large batch of dough and spinning it into flat pizza bases. Even when Cas succeeded to make one without dropping it, Yahoo pushed him on and on to keep trying.

"You got it, Man. But you need more practice."

He tossed him a lump of dough, then another until he was happy that Cas had the knack perfect.

Standing side by side at the work surface with a pizza base in front of them both, Cas copied exactly what Yahoo did including shouting out the name of each ingredient as they topped the pizzas.

The first two went into the oven.

"That was actually more fun than I expected," Cas said.

"Fun makes it much easier to learn and work. Now, be aware that they are cooking—you don't want to burn them, but don't wait around for them wasting time."

He grabbed another pizza base and Cas followed. The whole process started again with different ingredients.

"This one's for the vegetarians," Yahoo hollered.

Looking up and down the work bench, Cas had a question.

"There isn't any sweet corn on here. There's always sweet corn on the pizzas in the shop."

"That's because it's wrong. No one wants sweet corn on their pizza. Put the idea out of your head and get these recipes into it."

Yahoo continued arranging the pizza and repeating each ingredient three or four times. Deciding to keep his ideas to himself, Cas did the same.

"...Mushroom, OVEN!" Yahoo yelled.

Cas ran to the oven and took out the most perfect and delicious-looking pizzas he'd ever seen. He placed them on wooden plates on the work surface and took the two-handled cutter and held it over the pizza. Yahoo snatched it from him.

"Like this. They're getting cold."

Bang, bang, bang and the pizza was cut into six slices. He passed it to Cas and he did the same, almost as fast.

"Take them to you customers."

Understanding that Yahoo wasn't meaning to sound rude, but was teaching him the way that he was probably taught himself, he smiled and marched off with the pizzas. It was strange being behind the bar rather than in front. He placed one at the end where some of the footballers were standing and one at the other end where people were seated.

"Help yourselves, guys. There's more on the way."

The footballers' hands had already cleared the wooden board before he'd left the bar.

Popping the next two into the oven, Cas grabbed

another two balls and slapped then down in front of them. Lexy stuck her head round the door.

"Keep it up. They're all ringing their mates. I think we're in for a busy night."

"That's what I like to hear. Get back to your duties, Wench."

Cas chuckled. "You really know how to get into character."

"Tomato sauce."

"Tomato sauce."

Lexy smiled and went back where she belonged.

They continued in this way into the evening. Cas had learnt every recipe Yahoo had and his oven timing was as good as instinctual. Every pizza had been ravished, crusts and all.

Shaking Yahoo's hand, Cas couldn't stop himself from hugging him.

"Thank you so much. I'm gonna love this job."

"Good! Cos now you have to clean the whole place up while I go and have a beer."

"No problem. It's my pleasure."

"It's your job."

Quit

"What are you doing, Cas?" Yahoo asked, catching him unawares in the hallway.

"I thought I'd better go into work—just for today."

"Why?"

"In case Lexy doesn't pass the exam. I can't afford to lose that job. I'm being sensible, okay. I have every faith in her, but …"

"You have every faith in her—but. That's one big, fat contradiction. Here, call them and tell them you quit." Yahoo handed him his phone.

"I might as well go in. There's nothing else to do today until we hear from Lexy."

"But when we do hear, you've got an incredibly busy weekend ahead of you. Can you imagine how you'll feel sitting in that office this afternoon while me and Lexy know the outcome and you're trapped in there 'til hometime not knowing, one way or the other, what has happened. You can't do it. It will push you over the edge."

"I'll manage. If I quit and she fails, all I'll have is a pile of debt and no way of paying it back. I'm not just thinking of me—I'm thinking of everyone."

"Really? So, when Lexy rings me to tell us the good news, how do you think she's going to feel when I tell her you're at work? She won't think much of that. It could do a lot of damage to her confidence in you and herself. You can't go. You have to be here when she calls."

"I want to be here when she rings, but I'm caught in a horrid position."

Placing his body in the door frame, Yahoo spread his arms and legs out and tensed up.

"Now you don't have a choice. You could try climbing out the window, but you aren't getting out this way. Ring them else you're messing with my day too."

Cas called the office. It was ten minutes before he was supposed to swipe his hand in the scanner. Not being able to bring himself to quit, he blamed the doctor for telling him to have the rest of the week off. He guessed his illness excuse was taken with a hint of suspicion, as Wendy didn't speak with her sexy telephone voice.

"Done. I'm not going in. You can get out of the doorway. What are we going to do all day?"

"Something will come up. It always does. You didn't quit, though."

"I'll quit when we know for sure. I promise."

"I can't say I blame you really. It must be a worry owing me so much money." Yahoo winked.

"What do we do then? Sit around here waiting all day?"

"No, but we will take it easy. We'll go trout fishing and get a tan at the same time. Go and take that stuffy suit off and get into some chill-out clothes."

With the roof of the Audi down, they drove to the reservoir. Cas ducked down in his seat as they passed the sign for the car park. There was a possibility that the guys that battered him might still be lurking there.

They continued on safely and turned off the main road at the trout fishing sign.

"Have you ever been fishing?" Yahoo asked, as he

parked the car.

"Only when I was small. I've never been trout fishing. I know how to do a mean roast trout. It was one of Mum's favourites. The guy next door used to give us them regularly cos he didn't have enough room in his freezer. That reminds me—I was going to try and get home for Mum's birthday, but if Lexy pulls it off, I won't have time. I haven't even sent her a card."

"Don't worry about it. When you call her tonight and tell her your news, I'm sure she'll be over the moon and understand why you missed it. Now let's get a boat."

"A boat?"

"Yes, a boat. They aren't going to come to us. We have to find them—that's all part of the fun."

"I could believe, if you stood at the bank with a net, that they'd jump straight into it with your luck."

"Have you ever tried that, Cas?"

"No."

"So, how do you know they wouldn't jump in for you?"

"Point taken."

After collecting the equipment, they set out in the two-man rowing boat to the middle of the reservoir. Yahoo showed Cas the technique and caught a trout in the process.

They fished throughout the morning moving from one spot to another on Yahoo's intuition. Cas had a bite, but lost it before he'd got the fish close to the boat. He wasn't disappointed; he hadn't expected anything to even nibble at his hook.

Soon there were three large trout lying in the middle of the little boat, all caught by Yahoo, but Cas didn't mind a bit. The sun was warm, the trip relaxing and his mind was taken off the worry of Lexy passing her exam. Looking around at the idyllic landscape, he spotted some cars upon a hill. His eyes zoomed in on a silver Mini Coupe with a red roof and he put down his rod and took out his camera. Watching and waiting, he stayed calm. The boat jolted a little, but he didn't lose control.

"Holy shit! Are you filming it?" Yahoo announced.

"Oh, yes. I'm filming it alright," Cas replied with his back to Yahoo.

"Me too. This is my retirement video."

Staring at his camera, Cas couldn't see that anything was happening. He zoomed in further until the Mini was the only thing filling the screen. There was no movement at all. He couldn't even make out if there were figures in the car. The pair of them were silent for a good three minutes before Yahoo let out a scream.

"Yaaaaahooooo!"

Jumping up and down in the boat caused Cas to lose his frame.

"Stop jumping about. I'm trying to keep steady."

"But it's gone. What are you filming anyway? It was over there in front of the boat."

"What was?" Cas switched off the camera and turned to face Yahoo. Sitting face to face with the trout at their feet, Yahoo showed Cas his video.

"I don't know what it was. It's as big as a whale, but shaped like an eel—its neck was anyway. I've never seen anything like it before, but I'm happy to go with the Loch Ness monster. It's a bit far from home, but maybe it migrates in the summer. That is the best footage of it that I've ever seen. You did get some of it, didn't you?"

Cas looked blank and didn't answer, as Yahoo took the camera from him and watched what he'd recorded.

"Man, you really aren't cut out for this business."

They both cracked up laughing and then rowed back to the boatyard.

Back at the flat, Cas watched on as Yahoo edited all the best bits of his video together and highlighted the time and place of the sighting. His scream of Yahoo was placed cleverly throughout the footage to give his name as much exposure as possible and once he was happy with it, he called his contacts at news stations around the world.

Cas appreciated why Yahoo had been so pleased with himself for shooting this one. It was the clearest, longest and most genuine-looking video of a monster he'd ever seen. The only downside to the experience was that he had actually been there at the time and hadn't got to see it with his own eyes.

"Am I great?" Yahoo turned to him and asked once he'd finished.

"You are fantastic and deserve all the credit and money you make from that."

"Shall we take a look at Cas's efforts today?"

"Don't take the piss alright. I sensed there was something about to happen—I was just facing the wrong way. If I'd got in the boat first instead of you, it would have been a different story."

"But you didn't."

"I nearly did."

"Pfft."

Yahoo's mobile beeped interrupting their banter.

"It's a text from Lexy."

"And?"

"It just says 'Meet me at the pub' nothing else. Not even a kiss."

Jumping up, the pair of them ran out the flat. Yahoo cried out, "Yahoo," and punched the sky. Cas withstood the pain in his ankle to keep up with Yahoo, but he was not so confident about the message.

"It doesn't sound good to me. Surely, she'd have just

said—if it was good news."

"She's keeping us hanging. She wants to tell us face to face."

"I wish I felt the same. It sounded like she was upset to me."

"It was a text. It didn't sound at all. It's you that's negative. She wouldn't be at the pub if she'd failed. Get a grip and shake it off."

It was so easy for Yahoo to say these things. His future wasn't dangling on what was to come out of Lexy's mouth in the next few minutes. He'd get his money back and that would be the end of it. His success would continue while Cas would be stuck in that office and left to go mental.

Cas unlocked the door and they walked in to silence.

"Maybe we beat her to it," Yahoo said.

"Listen. That mooing noise. She's out the back with that mangy cat."

Walking through to the kitchen, the mooing got louder and so did the sobs.

Sitting on the doorstep stroking Two Bums, Lexy was crying.

They both stared in disappointment at the scene.

Yahoo sat down next to her and put his arm around her shoulder. Cas glanced around his perfect kitchen then slumped forwards onto the microwave and hid his face in his arms.

"Hey, it's okay, Gal. I'm sure they'll let you do a resit. You'll pass next time," Yahoo said.

"It's not the exam. I passed that. It's my boyfriend. He's dumped me." A wail left her mouth and a stream of snot left her nose.

Leaping up off the step, Yahoo pogoed around the kitchen crying out, "Yahoo."

He grabbed Cas around his waist, so he had no choice

but to hop around with him. It sank in they'd done it, but it didn't seem right to be so excited considering the situation. Forcing off Yahoo's grip, Cas escaped the dance.

"She's upset, Man. Can't you see that?"

"She'll get over it. She's better off without that oaf."

Two Bums had jumped up on her lap and Lexy seemed to calm as she stroked her. She turned to the boys.

"He was an oaf and you're right—I'm better off without him. I'm upset that he's been seeing someone else for months and he's chosen her over me. I know her and she's a right dog. What does that make me?"

Cas thought he would never understand women, so he didn't say a word.

Still on a high, Yahoo ruffled her hair. "You are beautiful and about to become a very successful business woman. What he's done says nothing about you—it only shows what a fool and a thick shit he is."

Lexy started laughing her head off.

Slightly confused, Cas realised there was a lot more to Yahoo than just his super-sense and that he had a lot to learn about people and the world.

Opening up her handbag, Lexy took out a photograph and ripped it in two. She threw it towards the bin, but missed.

As Cas bent down to put the pieces where they belonged, he recognised the face as one of his attackers from the night at the car park. His heart sank at the thought of that guy finding out that he had moved in with his ex-girlfriend the day after he'd dumped her. He envisaged yet another pummelling by the thug and wondered why even the good things that happened to him were tainted in some way. He tried his best not to let his angst show, as Lexy called the area manager to tell him the good news. Her eyes, now dry, widened with excitement and she grinned from ear to ear.

"We're open for business," she shouted, hugging both the guys. Then she scuttled off to set up the bar.

"Can I borrow your phone? I have to ring the office and tell them I won't be back," Cas said, flicking Two Bums away from the door with his foot and closing it.

"Sure." Yahoo handed him the phone and left him alone in the kitchen.

Nervous and with a slight sense of guilt for being ungrateful, Cas got through to Wendy.

"Hi, Wendy. How are you?"

"I'm fine. How are you?"

"I'm just calling to say something has come up and I won't be coming into work anymore. Like ever."

"I don't blame you. If I had the chance, I wouldn't come here ever again either. Good luck with whatever you're doing."

"Thanks. Bye, bye."

"Bye."

He wasn't expecting that, but it made it a lot easier for him. Now all he had to do was tell his mother and he had no idea what her reaction was going to be.

"Hi, Mum. It's Cas."

"Have you got a new phone? I've been trying to ring you, but nothing happens."

"No. I borrowed it—mine got um ... broken."

"Oh dear. You never were any good at looking after things."

"Don't worry about that. I've got some good news. I've quit that job and I'm going it alone. Well, in partnership, to be honest. I'm self-employed now."

"You gave up your job after two weeks? You've spent years trying to get a job and you throw it away after a fortnight? I can't believe you'd be so foolish. No! That's not true—I can believe it. Oh, Cas, why do you do these things to me?"

"Mother, listen. I am the Landlord of my own pub. Well, it's mine and Lexy's. She's the Landlady."

"You've got a wife in a fortnight?"

"No, no, no. It's not like that. She's my business partner—nothing more."

"I'd still like to meet her."

"Yes, you will. That's not why I'm calling. I'm letting you know where I am. I'm moving into the pub tomorrow. I'll email you the details."

"What's she like?"

"Who?"

"Lexy."

"What? She was a barmaid, but now she's the Landlady. Look, I have to go and make some dough."

"That's a good attitude you've picked up while being away."

"I mean dough, not … oh, it doesn't matter. I'd love you to come and visit sometime."

"Of course, don't forget to send me the details and send my love to Lexy."

"Will do. Bye, Mum."

"Bye, bye."

Finding Lexy making posters for an 'Under new management party', Cas finally realised it was real. This was really happening to him and all the trepidation, he had been suffering with, left his body. He was strong and optimistic about the venture, and filled with positive energy for the first time in his life. He noticed a change in Lexy too. She looked happy and the griping, dogsbody barmaid image that he'd encountered a fortnight ago was gone. She was thriving on being in charge and getting organised.

He passed the phone back to Yahoo.

"That's the end of the BEET Office."

"Feels good, yeah?"

"Very."

"What time are you opening today?"

Lexy was sticking a poster in the window.

"Now, but keep it quiet about us for tonight. It'll cause plenty of gossip and intrigue and we'll reveal all tomorrow night at the party."

"Sounds like a great idea. I'll leave you to it—I've got work to do myself."

Yahoo left, latching the front door open.

Returning to the kitchen, Cas prepared dough and tomato sauce, as Lexy did what she did best and fronted the bar.

The evening went without a hitch and each time Cas delivered a pizza to a table, he was badgered and questioned about what had happened to the last Landlord and who was taking over.

Acting none the wiser, he shrugged his shoulders.

"I'm not sure what's happening. We'll find out tomorrow night, I guess."

At least he had his kitchen to retreat to away from them all. Checking out how Lexy was coping with the constant prying, he saw that she was having a great time playing the insecure barmaid who was always the last to be told anything. Members of the winning quiz team where bothering them both throughout the evening. Cas found their annoyance, of not knowing what was going on, highly amusing.

Hearing the familiar mooing at the back door, he placed a bowl of tuna on the step. Even Two Bums didn't seem so bad anymore.

Returning to Yahoo's flat for the last time, at two in the

morning, he packed his case for the second time. He could hear Yahoo snoring and wondered what he'd been working on that evening.

'I'll have a look in the morning. It's bound to be a cracker,' he thought and went to bed.

Move

When Cas woke up, he found the flat empty to his dismay. He was looking forward to spending a little time with the guy, who had done so much for him, before he walked out of the place for the last time. It was the way Yahoo was though, and if he had a hunch, he would be gone without an idea of when he'd return. So with a couple of hours to kill before he needed to be at the pub, he thought he'd go shopping for a new phone and maybe a house-warming present for Lexy with the little money he had left.

On the corner at the crossroads near the phone shop, he found himself standing next to The Krankies Mini. Mrs. Krankie was waiting in the passenger seat with the window wound down. Cas waved to her and smiled and she stuck her thumb up and laughed.

He went into the shop and bought a new phone. When he left, the Mini Coupe was gone.

'It was a ludicrous idea,' he told himself, as he counted the last little bit of money that remained from the wad his mother had given him. He wasn't going to get Lexy much of a present. In a world of his own, as he pondered on what she would like, he found himself staring into the window of a pet shop.

'She likes animals and I must have enough for a goldfish.' He remembered what his mother had said about always having a little life in the house and it seemed the perfect choice.

He went in and scanned the rows of tanks for something with a bit of character. Spotting a goldfish with big bulbous eyes and black markings that created the illusion of a handlebar moustache, he knew that was the one for her.

"I'd like a fish, please," he said to the assistant.

"Any particular fish?"

"Yes. The black and orange one with the big eyes."

"Do you have a water sample?"

"I'm sorry?"

"You have to bring a water sample for me to test."

"Is this a pet shop or a doctor's surgery?"

The woman didn't look at all impressed by his reply.

"A water sample that the fish is going to live in. We have rules for the animals' welfare and if you don't have a suitable water sample—you don't get a fish."

"Okay, I'll go and buy a bottle of water."

"It can't be any old water. You have to set up the environment and the water has to be left for at least two days. It needs to have been oxygenated and you can buy a solution from us to get the correct Ph balance. Then, bring in the water and I'll test it."

"What! It's a God-damn fish. My mum's had a fish for as long as I can remember. It's probably older than me and she refills the bowl with tap water. The fish is fine."

"It's probably incredibly stressed, but how would you know? And if that's your attitude, then I'm sorry, but I will not be selling you a fish EVER!"

"Fine! Stuff the fish," Cas said, marching out of the shop.

He'd become a Landlord of a pub that he'd only clapped eyes on a fortnight ago, yet he couldn't do something as simple as buying a goldfish. The world didn't make any sense to him.

There was no time left for present hunting; he had to go and fetch his case and get to the pub.

Still no sign of Yahoo in the flat, Cas was disappointed to leave without saying thank you and good bye, but time wasn't on his side to be waiting around. He took his case and the bag of trout, paused on the doorstep for a little while before locking the door and sticking the keys through the letterbox.

"Good bye."

He walked to his new home and let himself in.

"Lexy!" he called.

"I'm upstairs. This place is a dump."

Taking the trout through to the kitchen, he squeezed them into the overcrowded fridge and noticed that a huge freezer had been delivered. He removed the packaging and plugged it in. It was yet another thing to be grateful to Yahoo for.

Humping his suitcase up the stairs he could smell a mixture of bad odours. Damp, sweat, tobacco and rotten food drifted past him. At the top, he was hit with a strong whiff of bleach.

Greeting him in pink rubber gloves, Lexy shook her head.

"Hiya! I honestly don't know how that man could have lived like this. I know he was a lazy arse, but nothing looks like it's been cleaned for years. It won't take me long to make it habitable, but we will have to do some decorating at some point. I can't live with the seventies wallpaper. Come on, I'll show you the rooms."

There were five bedrooms and Lexy pointed to the smallest.

"I thought we could use this one as an office. If we're

going to run this place properly, we'll need a proper office."

Cas nodded. He wasn't quite sure what they would need an office for, but it was nice to know that his partner seemed to have some idea.

"I'm having this room, so you have the choice of those three. I was thinking about security and as I'm at the front of the pub, I thought it would make sense if you were at the back. That way if anyone tries to break in, we have more chance of hearing them—until we get an alarm installed, that is. I've arranged for someone to come this week and give us a quote."

"That makes perfect sense. I'll take the back one." He was more than surprised at Lexy's efficiency. She was way ahead of him. To think he was going to turn up with a suitcase, some dead fish, a goldfish and just settle in, made him slightly ridiculous. Being refused the goldfish was the best thing that could have happened.

The room was a far cry from the room he'd just vacated. There was a bed, a wardrobe and a set of drawers with three legs and a breeze block in the place of the forth leg.

Putting the suitcase on the bed, he began to unpack. Lexy appeared with a pile of bedding.

"I bought duvets and stuff, but you can make your own bed," she said, throwing them down and she left him to it.

He smiled to himself. She still had that Lexy spark, but had also thought of everything. It's a shame he wasn't so 'on the ball', but he had been thrown in at the deep end and wasn't even sure how he got there. The previous few days were a blur. He had a new job and a new home. Making a promise to himself that he was going to work hard and prove to everyone that they were right to have faith in him, he recognised that it was his own lack of faith in himself that had hindered his ability to take the whole thing seriously.

His case unpacked, he swung it up onto the top of the wardrobe and whispered to it, "I won't be needing you for a long time."

Hearing mooing from outside, Cas went to the window and looked down. His room was directly over the backdoor of the kitchen. He wondered how long before Bob was discharged, as he wouldn't be sleeping if he had to listen to that racket all night.

It was time to work.

Down in the kitchen, he placed a huge bowl on the side to prepare dough. Lexy called him from the bar.

"What do you think? This should say it all and stop the rumours."

Poking his head round into the bar, he looked around the room, but couldn't see anything different except a step ladder.

"What's the point of that?"

"Come round here—like you've just walked in."

Walking round to where she was standing, he couldn't miss the banner displayed across the top of the bar.

It read, 'Lexy and Cass welcome you to The White Horse.'

"Well? Isn't it great? Now everyone will know it's ours," Lexy squealed.

"Cas has one S. That's the girls' way of spelling it."

"Does it matter? They'll get the message."

"I suppose not."

"Oh, for God's sake. If it's going to make you grumpy ..." She climbed up the ladder and drew a big cross through the second S. "Happy now?"

"Yeah."

"Look, later when you're not busy, I want you behind

the bar too. You can practise pulling pints and get to know the customers—assert yourself as the Landlord and all that."

Although Cas was taken aback by the very thought of being pushed into the limelight and asserting himself, he didn't let it show. He'd do it because he had to; there was no choice.

While Lexy was opening the doors, Cas took the step ladder out the back and prepared his kitchen. His nerves soon calmed, as time after time, Lexy called him through to the bar to be congratulated by the nosy patrons. When the lunchtime rush for pizzas was over, he was well accustomed to standing on the wrong side of the bar. Pulling pints didn't come naturally, but Lexy stood close and whispered tips in his ear.

"Hold the glass further down, near the base -
Never put your finger inside the glass -
Not that glass. He has a jug -
He likes the lemonade in the bottom -
He likes the lemonade in the top -
Don't even bother trying to pour a Guinness. Give it here."

To both of their surprise, guys with instruments and speakers came through the door and started setting them up in the corner.

Lexy nudged Cas. "Go and see what's going on then."

Clearing his throat, Cas walked over to the musicians.

"Hello. What are you doing?"

"We've been booked for tonight. A guy called Yahoo or something!"

"Of course. Carry on."

He scuttled back to the bar.

"It's okay. Yahoo organised it - they're bound to be good."

Lexy clapped her hands.

"Bob's waiting to be served," she whispered.

Looking round, there was Bob at the bar.

"He drinks Guinness. You told me not to pour Guinness."

"You can still ask him what he'd like. I'll pour it."

Nervously, Cas walked over to Bob.

"Your usual, Bob?"

"That would be much appreciated. I want to apologise to you, Cas."

"Don't worry about it. It's water under the bridge. I hope you're feeling better after your, um ... little rest. We've been looking after the cat and I'm sure she'll be pleased that you're home."

"It's a HE. Haven't I explained that to you?"

"Yes. Of course, I'm sorry."

Lexy seemed to be taking ages with the Guinness, but the conversation was interrupted as Yahoo entered the pub. He held his arms in the air.

"Surprise! Surprise!"

He stepped aside of the door holding it open and in walked Cas's mum. She was carrying a large bowl with a goldfish in it.

"Mum!" Cas ran around from the bar to greet his mother. Taking the bowl from her and placing it on the bar, he turned and hugged her.

"How did you get here and with that?"

"Yahoo called me last night and arranged to pick me up today. We thought it would be a nice surprise and I couldn't wait to see if what you told me was true."

"And the fish?"

"I didn't come all the way here with it on my lap, silly. We bought it a little while ago and set it up at Yahoo's flat. You should always have something alive in your home,

Son."

"I know. If you knew the trouble I've been to—trying to buy a fish."

"It was no trouble. The woman was happy to sell me it. She said it would serve the arse right. Apparently, some foolish lad had wanted it earlier on. She didn't like his attitude and was hoping to get shot of the fish before he came back."

"She sold you it without a water sample?"

"Oh no! I always carry a water sample in my handbag—I just can't do it on demand when the doctor asks. I couldn't see why she needed it to sell me a fish, but she seemed happy enough with it."

Cas looked into the bowl. The boggle-eyed fish with a handlebar moustache stared back at him.

"He's very unusual. I've never seen a fish like that before." He lied.

Leaning over, Bob studied the fish.

"It's a female. You can tell by its tail."

"Whatever, Bob. I'll take it out of the way before someone knocks it over or drinks it. Sit down, Mum. Lexy will get you a drink."

As he carried the bowl through to the stairwell, he could hear his mother.

"So, you're the mysterious Landlady in his life."

"Oh, Mother," he muttered, as he took his fish up the stairs and was out of ear shot.

Placing the bowl on the coffee table in the living room, he noticed that the book and the die were still there where the last Landlord had left them.

After what had happened to Bob, he had no intentions of reading the book himself. He also didn't want Lexy losing her head because of it either and thought it best to return it to its rightful owner. He realised the shock of Bob seeing the book again might trigger another episode, but it was his book, so Cas decided to ask him first and bin it if he didn't want it.

He placed it on the bottom stair and went through to the bar.

"Bob. The book you leant us. Do you want it back?"

Mother interrupted.

"Well, of course he'll want it back if he leant you it, Son. What's wrong with your manners?"

Wildly, Bob shook his head.

"I don't want it back. I don't want to see it ever again. Burn it if you have to."

Cas's mum was appalled.

"You should never burn books. Give it to a charity shop or pass it on, but don't ever burn books. I'll take it if it's inconvenient for you, Cas."

Backing away, Cas left the two of them to discuss why book burning was such a crime and why Bob felt so strongly about that particular book. He sidled his way down to where Yahoo was standing.

"That was a great surprise, Mate. You really are the best. When are you taking her home?"

"Tomorrow, after my free super-sized Sunday roast. I said she could stay in your old room tonight if you don't have room here."

"We've got enough room, but the place is pretty grotty. We'll leave her to decide—she will anyway."

"How many rooms have you got up there?"

"Five bedrooms—two spare."

"Well, if I were you, I'd get those spare ones done up. I've heard there are people flocking here from all over the world because of that Loch Ness monster video. They're going to need places to stay and they're few and far between in this town."

"Really? I'll get to it after the weekend. I'd be stupid to leave them empty."

"That's what I like to hear, Cas. You're starting to sound more like a businessman minute by minute."

Cas frowned at the glass in Yahoo's hand. "What's with the orange juice? We're having a party, Man."

"The car's outside and I have a feeling I might be needing it. I'll stay on the safe side of the law for now."

Red fingernails appeared on Yahoo's shoulders before Wendy's face popped up from behind him.

"So! This is what you're up to, Cas."

Apart from a pang of ungratefulness, Cas was pleased that she'd sussed him out. He was proud that he'd got out of that place in a fortnight. He nodded and smiled, but she was more interested in his mate than his reply.

"And how's the gorgeous, Yahoo?" she said in the most exaggerated sexy voice Cas had heard so far.

"I'm good, Wendy. I see you're still trying to get your claws into anything with a deeper voice than yourself."

Her hand flicked away from his shoulder and pretended she hadn't heard his comment.

"House vodka, Lexy."

The band started playing and no one could be heard. Cas did his best to memorise who was drinking what and lip reading anyone he wasn't sure of. The pizza menus were put away at eight. He was too busy to be in both places at once and realised that if this was how things were to carry on, they would have to employ some bar-staff. He chuckled to himself, as he found it amusing that he would be someone's boss. He, who had only ever been an employee for less than two weeks.

Noticing that they were running out of clean glasses behind the bar, Cas didn't wait to be told and went out among the happy customers and collected some up. He was gob-smacked to see The Krankies walk in, straight past him and up to the bar. He watched as Lexy served them orange juices and he realised how crazy his life really was. All that time he'd spent looking for them and pursuing them and now that he'd given up on the idea, they'd both walked into his bar. He watched them as they greeted Bob, their old postman, and even got chatting with his mother.

Putting down an armful of glasses on the end of the bar, he went back for more. As he crossed in front of the band, Wendy gyrated her hips against him and shouted in his ear.

"Fancy a dance, Landlord?"

"No, but I would like to know how you knew that the Krankies go dogging."

Her mouth opened really wide and then she laughed hysterically making her way to a stool and sitting down holding her crotch, as if she was about to wet her pants. She beckoned Cas over. The band put down their instruments and went to the bar for a break and she explained why she found what he'd said so amusing.

"'The Krankies Go Dogging' is a play that my brother's am-dram group were performing. I didn't mean I'd seen those two doing, well, you know ... I can get you some tickets if you like. It's about this journalist who can't get a scoop—well, he hears this rumour and decides ..."

Cas interrupted, "I think I know how it goes. Don't spoil it for me."

She split into fits of laughter again, "... but it wouldn't surprise me if they did."

Walking away, Cas couldn't believe how foolish he'd been. He'd almost got himself killed and all because of a misunderstanding. Back behind the bar he tried to laugh it off.

Wendy snuck back up behind Yahoo and cupped her hand around his ear. Although Cas couldn't hear the conversation, he had an idea of what she might be saying, as he watched her slink off with the giggles. Yahoo hadn't found it funny; he was in deep thought by the looks of it.

The Krankies had taken over the microphone and had the place in fits of laughter. The band seemed happy for them to carry on for a good hour while they supped beer at the bar. Eventually, Jimmy Krankie put down the microphone and shouted, "Thank you!"

A huge cheer filled the room and cries of, "More."

"Sorry. We have to go. Things to do." Jimmy winked and waved as they left.

Another roar from the crowd and it all went flatly silent. The band went back to their instruments. Cas turned to Yahoo, but before he could speak, Yahoo was walking away.

"Yahoo!" Cas called.

"Things to do. See you later." Yahoo winked at him, but didn't stop.

Cas had an idea where he was going, but shrugged it off as coincidence.

As Yahoo walked out of the door, the football team walked in, dressed as real people and already half-cut. They cheered when they saw the banner and sang a song about Lexy being the boss with tits.

She happily served them before turning to Cas and whispering, "It's going to be a long night, but we're making a fortune."

The music, dancing and partying continued. Realising it was way past his mother's usual bedtime, Cas went to see how she was. She looked quite cosy sitting with Bob, at his usual table near the corner, clapping her hands along to the music.

"Are you okay, Mum? I don't know what time Yahoo will be back, but I'll make a bed up here for you if you're tired," he shouted.

"I'm having a great time. I'll let you know when I've had enough. Don't you worry? Look what Bob got me." She held up a photo of the Krankies with their autograph on it.

"That's lovely." Cas didn't think his mother was really a fan of the Krankies. He'd made that up to find their address, but she seemed very pleased with it. Maybe she was just being polite.

Bob beckoned him in.

"I hope you don't mind, Cas. I know you wanted to give it to her, but they were standing right there and she saw me get it signed to her."

"Don't worry, Bob. It's a lovely thought."

Cas was worried, though. He was unsure of how stable Bob was. He hadn't had that much time to talk to him and he was wary that Bob might try and sneak his mother home with him. It was a relief to see him rise and walk out of the door alone only moments later. Perhaps he'd sensed Cas's concern and had done the gentlemanly thing.

Not long after, his mother collared him.

"Cas," she shouted, way too loudly in his ear, "I'm pooped."

"Come on then. I'll show you to your room."

As they walked up the stairs, she seemed to be crying.

"What's wrong? Did that Bob do something to upset you?"

"No. Not at all. I'm just so happy for you, so proud of you and I've had a fantastic night."

Hugging her, he replied, "Good. I thought he'd ... well ... you never know, do you?"

"Oh, don't be so silly. He was nothing but a gentleman.

He told me all about his breakdown and it was due to suppressing his grief. He's getting the right treatment for it now. He's fine. He's invited me out for Sunday dinner tomorrow."

"What? No, Mum. Please don't go. Please, I beg you. You're here to visit me. I want you here tomorrow."

"That's exactly where I intend to be. We're having Sunday dinner here. That's what you're advertising, aren't you? You don't think I'm daft enough to go off somewhere with someone I've only just met do you? You should know me better than that."

Cas's heart had almost stopped when she'd said that she was going for dinner. He was so relieved that his mother had more sense than he had when he'd first arrived. To his surprise, Lexy had made up the spare bedroom with new bedding. That saved him a job. He kissed his mother on the cheek and left her there. Lexy was rushed off her feet and Cas got stuck in again to help out.

The footballers were getting rowdy and trying to outdo the band with their singing. Even though the band had speakers, they were no match for them and the singer threw down his mike in temper and stormed over to the bar.

"Can't you do something? They're ruining my performance."

"Give me a minute," Cas replied and shuffled along to Lexy.

"The band is getting the arse with the footballers. They want me to do something. I'm not sure what to do."

"Think about it."

"What? The guy's standing there telling me to do something. I'm not going to tell him—I'm thinking about it."

"The band is being paid. The band doesn't drink in this pub. The footballers are paying us and they regularly drink here—I agree they are rowdy, but they know all the other customers who follow them and want them to bring back trophies for their pub. Who would you rather upset?"

"I don't want to upset anyone."

Their first business discussion was interrupted by a huge voice.

"Excuse me! Excuse me!"

The room went very quiet. Even the footballers shut up.

Cas turned to the lady at the bar.

"Can I help you?"

"I left my costume here last week. I want it back."

The guy from the band had lost his patience and told the rest of them to start packing away their kit.

Cas hadn't a clue who the woman was, but Lexy recognised her.

"I know where it is. Give me a minute."

The woman waited, staring from face to face around the room. One by one, the footballers drank their drinks and left.

Returning with a carrier bag, Lexy handed it to the woman.

"It's as it was when you left it. I thought you'd be back for it, so I put it out of harm's way."

"Thank you, Dear! Were those boys the Umpa Lumpas?"

"No. I haven't seen those fools since." Lexy lied.

"Okay. Thanks again. Bye."

Cas realised who the woman was and he'd never have recognised her from the video he'd seen at Yahoo's flat. He was amazed at how the whole thing had panned out and how Lexy had handled it without upsetting or losing a single customer. He did still have a lot to learn, but as he'd always said, he was a fast learner.

With the band packed up and leaving, the remaining customers supped up and made off.

"If it carries on at this rate, we're gonna need staff," Cas said.

"You read my mind, but for now, we'll have to cope on our own. I'll cash up—you go to bed. You've got a hell of a lot to do in the morning."

"Too right I have. Good night."

"Good night."

Roast

Rising to the mooing demands of Two Bums outside his window, Cas knew exactly where he was and how much work he had to do that morning.

Leaving his mother and Lexy to sleep, he went down to the kitchen and turned on the radio to drown out the noise from the cat. After two cups of coffee, he began the preparations for Sunday dinner.

Serious things filled his head as he worked. They would definitely have to get some staff sometime soon. He would look on the internet and make sure he did it all legit. There was so much he didn't know about business and how things worked that he promised himself he'd research it all in the week ahead when they were less busy. They needed to get an accountant too. He'd make a point of asking around and getting a good one. He also had to learn to drive. It wasn't fair to have to get Yahoo to take him everywhere and although Lexy could drive, she had enough to do without hunting for the best ingredients. There was decorating to do too and the two guest rooms were his first priority. He decided to start sorting out all these things as soon as possible. He'd never been more motivated in his whole life, as he was at that moment, peeling carrots and preparing the trout.

Lexy was the first to emerge from the flat.

"Do you want a hand with anything?"

"No. You sit down. I'll make you a coffee."

"Good. Cos I've got enough to do."

"Not a morning person, are you?" Cas handed her a cup of coffee.

"Luckily not. You need to be a night person in this job."

"It was a good night, though—wasn't it? Takings-wise."

"It was the best night I've seen since I've worked here. I'm going to have to get an extra delivery. What we've got left isn't going to last us until Thursday or even Tuesday at this rate. Not that I'm complaining."

"You could have fooled me."

"I'm going to clean the pub. See you later."

By the time his mother appeared, Cas had everything roasting and simmering away and two more lots ready to go in as soon as the first would be ready for serving.

"Coffee, Mum?"

"I'd love one. Where's the milk pan?"

"It's a machine, Mum. It comes out however you want it. There's no room for a milk pan anyway."

He pressed the machine and made her a cup that he hoped would suit her.

"Here."

"Wow! That was quick. I might have to get one of those."

That was one thing Cas never thought he'd hear his mother say.

"I'm sure you'll enjoy it."

"It tastes lovely. I'll go through to the bar and save myself a table. I've got a feeling you're going to be very busy today."

She took her coffee through to the bar. Cas was glad she hadn't interfered in his kitchen. It was just like the Sundays back home.

Cas heard the bolts unlocking on the front door and got

ready for action.

The customers were numerous, but at a steady flow. He kept on top of everything, as if he'd been doing it for years. It wasn't that much different to a normal Sunday for him. A grander scale, but simpler than he'd expected.

By three o'clock, the orders lessened and he went to join his mother and Bob.

"How was it?"

"Delicious as ever and always better when someone else cooks it," his mother replied.

Bob rubbed his tummy. "It was very good indeed. I'll be coming here every week. I don't eat properly, otherwise. You wouldn't have any scraps for my cat would you? I haven't seen him since I've been home. Maybe if I put something out, he'll come back."

"I'll get you enough to last him the week. It is the least I can do," Cas said, heading off for a bag of scraps, before he'd hardly finished his sentence.

In the kitchen, Cas could hear Two Bums at the door, but he had no intention of feeding her another morsel. He carried a large bag of food back out to Bob. Yahoo had appeared and was sitting at their table.

"Where's my dinner?"

Cas held out the bag. "Here."

"Oh, don't tell me you've finished. I've been really busy all day. I shot something remarkable last night and today ..."

"Yahoo, later. My mother!"

"Oh, sorry."

Cas handed the bag to Bob.

"I'll get your dinner, Yahoo. You can tell me later."

When Cas returned with the dinner, Bob had already said his goodbyes and left.

"He is a very troubled man, but his heart's in the right

place," Cas's mum said.

"Don't worry about him, Mum. He pops in here every afternoon, so we'll keep an eye on him."

Cas could see the speed Yahoo was scoffing his dinner and he didn't want his mum to see his bad habit of licking the plate. She thought his new friend was wonderful and Cas wanted to keep it that way.

"I'm sure Yahoo has a lot to do today, Mum. Have you got everything?"

"I'll just pop upstairs and get my bag."

She disappeared in time to miss Yahoo wiping the plate around his face like he hadn't eaten in months.

"That was the best Sunday roast I've ever had."

Lexy took the plate from his hand. "That's probably because it was free."

"You haven't changed a bit. I'm glad this boss thing hasn't gone to your head, Wench."

"You're welcome," she said, as she banged the plate on the top of his head and walked away.

"Yahoo, I've got a new phone—I'll give you my number, what's yours?"

Cas tapped in the numbers and called Yahoo's phone.

Fiddling with his phone for a few seconds, Yahoo replied, "Got it, Mate. I did get your old one looked at, but it was way beyond repair. I managed to extract something interesting from it, though."

"Really! What?"

"You've got some dodgy footage on there of Lexy's ex with his trousers down. I knew I recognised him when he was beating you up, but I couldn't think where from. When I saw the video, I realised who it was."

Blushing, Cas shook his head.

"Just get rid of it, Mate. I was in the wrong place at the wrong time."

"No way! The woman he was with is one of my neighbours and she's married and on the neighbourhood Watch committee. It could be really useful to you if he ever decides to cause you any grief or she tries interfering or complaining about the noise."

"Nice one. Don't mention it to Lexy, though."

"Now, do you wanna see something amazing? It's the funniest, weirdest sight ever," Yahoo said, lifting his phone.

Cas put his hand over the mobile.

"Not now. My mum's coming. Thank you for bringing her and taking her back. You'd better get off or it'll take you all night."

Mum and Lexy hugged and said their goodbyes.

Cas went outside with them and saw Yahoo's scooter, looking as good as new, parked next to the door. It had a new paint job with 'Yahoo! Pizza!' splattered across each side and a carrier box on the back. Cas looked confused.

"You're not taking her home on that, are you?"

"Don't be daft. That's a present for you. I'm never going to ride her again and she'll only die being stuck in that garage forever. Try to look after her. She's the first of your fleet."

"I will, Mate. Thank you."

He hugged Yahoo and then his mother.

"It's a beautiful afternoon to be driving with the top down. I bet you feel like a film star, Mum."

"Indeed I do. I'm so proud of you, Son."

"Come visit whenever you like. I can't see that I'll have much time to get away from here myself."

She gave him a big kiss.

"Bye, bye, Son."

"I love you, Mum."

"I love you, too. Don't forget to feed the goldfish."

"I'll do it now."

"I love you too," Yahoo shouted as he pulled away.

It was sad to see his mother go, but Cas knew she'd be okay. She had a wise head on her shoulders and he was glad that he'd finally made her proud.

As he went through the kitchen, he smiled at the silence. The awful mooing had stopped. He went up the stairs to feed the goldfish.

"At least I don't have to wash up after you." He chuckled to himself, as he sprinkled in the fish food.

As he went back, down the stairs, he noticed Bob's book was gone from the bottom step. He was sure that that was where he'd left it and it had definitely been there that morning. He guessed, wrongly, that Lexy must have thrown it away.

Printed in Great Britain
by Amazon.co.uk, Ltd.,
Marston Gate.